LINGERING TOUCH

Other Works
CRAFTING A WRITER'S LIFE: Building a Foundation

Coming Soon

The Blades of Janus
PERIHELION

The Department of Homeworld Security
Nothing to Declare

Duration of Stay

The Department of Homeworld
Security
Book Six

Cassandra Chandler

Copyright Page

This book is pure fiction. All characters, places, names, and events are products of the author's imagination or used solely in a fictitious manner. Any resemblance to any people, places, things, or events that have ever existed or will ever exist is entirely coincidental.

Duration of Stay
The Department of Homeworld Security, Book Six
Copyright © 2017 by Cassandra Chandler
Print ISBN: 978-1-945702-37-2
Digital ISBN: 978-1-945702-25-9

First eBook edition: August 2017
First print edition: December 2018
10 9 8 7 6 5 4 3 2 1

cassandra-chandler.com
P.O. Box 91
Mission, Kansas 66201

Dedication

For Joey N.—my writing bestie.

Don't miss out on any of the alien action.
Subscribe to Cassandra Chandler's newsletter at
cassandra-chandler.com!

Chapter One

The windows of Brooke's car were covered in fog. If she'd been sitting inside—maybe drinking one of the gazillion hot drinks she'd made for customers that day—it would make sense. But she was just getting off her shift, and her car had been parked in the nearly empty lot for hours.

"Elliot, you asshole," Brooke said. "Get out of my car and give me back my spare key."

Not that he'd need it to get in later. He knew that the back driver's side door didn't lock right anymore. She lined up her keys between her fingers, making sure the sharp edges pointed out like claws. He'd only been incredibly annoying since the breakup, but she wanted to be ready in case he'd finally gone off the deep end.

She jerked open the door and let out a disgusted grunt. He was lying sort of curled up in the footwell, his dark hair masking his face.

"Seriously, this is reaching entirely new levels of pathetic. It's been three months. Get over it."

A sudden feeling of misgiving shivered through her. Had

he cut his hair? And had he always been that tall? And buff?

Her car was a piece of crap, but it was spacious. And he was suddenly taking up every inch of the available space.

His legs were bent and he was hunched over with his arms wrapped around his torso. Her skin felt electrified as she realized that whoever this guy sleeping in the back seat of her car was, he wasn't Elliot.

She raised her key-studded hand. "What are you doing in my car?"

The man lifted his head and turned to look at her. Her heart thudded in her chest.

His dark hair was a little longer at the front, dusting across his forehead. It was short in the back—nothing getting in the way of her view of his shoulders, which were massive. He had a long, straight nose, perfectly curved lips, honey-brown eyes, and an angular jaw covered in a thick coat of stubble. He was absolutely gorgeous.

The sweat coating his skin glistened faintly in the dim light. Why was he sweating when all he had on was a pair of jeans and a flannel shirt? He wasn't even wearing shoes.

She lowered her arm and stepped forward, poking her head into the back seat of her car. "Are you okay?"

He was shaking violently, his whole body trembling. He held up a hand to her and his sleeve fell back enough for her to see his corded forearm—and the line of silver light circling it. His skin was *glowing*.

"I won't hurt you," he said.

His voice sent a frisson through her. It was deep and strong, even with the obvious strain in it. Who the heck was this guy? *What* was he?

"You need help," she said.

"No doctors."

"Duh."

She slammed the door and quickly climbed into the driver's seat. It took several tries, but her decrepit car finally started. She had almost walked that morning, but it was too cold even for the couple of blocks between her home and work. Before putting the car in gear, she looked over the bench seat into the back.

"Do you promise you won't try to eat my face off?" she said.

"I won't try to eat your face off." He looked vaguely insulted at the idea. The furrows between his eyebrows deepened.

Crap, even his forehead was sexy. How was that possible?

"Or anything else?" she asked.

"I'm not going to eat you." This time, there was definite frustration in his tone.

"Okay."

She turned back around and took a deep breath, then exhaled. This was like something out of a movie. Hopefully not a horror flick.

As she pulled out of the parking lot, she said, "So what are you? A ghost? Fallen angel?"

"Scorpiian."

"What, like a bug?"

"I'm from Scorpii-2."

"Is that a company or something? Are you an android?" The silver glow could be some kind of LEDs in his body.

He let out a frustrated grunt. "It's a planet in the Scorpii system."

"Oh my God. You're an alien."

"Yeah."

An alien. In the back seat of her car.

"Are you having some kind of allergic reaction to our planet?"

"What? Why would I…"

"No offense, but you don't look so good."

She turned into the parking lot for her apartment complex. Luckily, there was a spot right next to the stairs up to her apartment. At midday in the middle of the week, no one was around.

"I mean, you look hot," she said. "But you also look… hot."

"Thanks for clarifying."

She ignored the crack, though she was glad to know he understood sarcasm. That would make it easier to communicate.

"Are you supposed to glow like that?" she said.

"No." He let out a groan and she heard him shift around more.

"Crap, you're not dying, are you?"

She set the parking brake, but didn't turn off the engine. She understood his desire to avoid any organization that might stuff him in a lab and experiment on him, but if it was a choice between that or death, he might have to reconsider the whole "no doctors" thing.

"I'm not dying. I'm acclimating."

"So it *is* some kind of reaction."

He let out another frustrated sigh. It was easier to handle than the little pain noise he'd made.

She stepped out into the frigid air, keeping her apartment key ready and wondering how she was going to get him up the stairs.

"Mom always said I was a rescuer," Brooke murmured. "If she could see me now."

The alien had managed to get himself out of the footwell and onto the back seat. He was dragging himself across the bench toward her. She opened his door and reached in to help him. His skin was burning hot.

"You have a fever," she said.

"I'm acclimating."

"Right. Whatever." She draped his arm over her shoulder and shut both car doors. "Let's go."

He started to pull away from her, veering toward the mound of snow piled at the edge of the lot. "I need to lower my body temperature."

"If someone sees you lying in a pile of snow, they'll call the cops."

Especially since he was still glowing. She could see more lines now that he was up—soft silver light gleaming around his neck, shoulders, and arms. There were even dim circles around his thighs that she could see faintly through his jeans.

He let her take the lead, though he stumbled a few times. It seemed like he was mostly able to support his own weight, which was helpful. All that muscle would make him way too heavy for her to drag up the stairs. They made it up to her apartment without drawing any attention, and she unlocked the door and helped him inside.

She slid the deadbolts and chain into place, just in case Elliot decided to show up unannounced—again. He needed to give her back her damned spare keys. If he walked in on Brooke while another guy was there… She didn't have the energy to handle the tantrum he'd throw.

She led the alien hottie further into her place. "The bathroom's over here."

"My body doesn't eliminate waste the way human bodies do," he said.

"Ew, really? Do you eat?"

He didn't answer her, probably because his body had started trembling violently again. If lowering his body temperature was necessary, they needed to get on that right away.

There were a lot of ways she'd like to get on his body, alien or not.

She dragged her attention back to the task at hand, pushing the other thoughts away. She was supposed to be helping the poor guy, not drooling over him. She kicked open the door to the bathroom.

"We need to get you in the tub. I can get snow from outside to help you cool down." She leaned him against a wall, then plugged the drain and started the cold water running.

When she turned back to him, he'd already unbuttoned his shirt. He was even more built than she'd thought. His chest was broad, without an ounce of extra fat. His abdomen rippled with muscle, and dark hair cascaded down his chest and belly, disappearing into his jeans.

"I'm trapped in this human form," he said.

"I can think of worse fates than being trapped in *this* one."

His shirt tangled around his arms as he tried to pull it off. He leaned heavily against the wall, as if just unbuttoning it had exhausted him. Lines of silver traced down the chiseled muscles of his abdomen, but they weren't smooth, as she'd thought earlier. They were jagged, almost like scars. But if they were scars, it looked like he'd been torn limb from limb and reassembled.

"Vapor pits," he said.

She shook her head. "I don't understand. Do you need some vapor pits or something?" Not that she had any idea what that was.

"It's a…" He let out an aggravated grunt. "I'm angry."

"Oh, it's a swear." When he stared at her blankly, she said, "Next time, try, 'fuck' or 'dammit'."

He glared at her, then tugged at his shirt.

"Let me help you." She peeled the shirt down the knotted muscle of his arms and then tossed it aside. As he braced himself against the wall, she reached around and unfastened his jeans.

"Normally, I can just form whatever clothing I need," he said. "This external material is impossible to manage."

"So, you're some kind of shapeshifting alien?"

He grunted. It wasn't a denial.

"You picked a good look."

She tugged his jeans past an ass that could be put on display in a museum, then dragged them over legs that surpassed her wildest fantasies. He had just the right amount of hair covering his perfectly sculpted thighs and toned calves.

He stepped into the water as soon as he was free of his clothes, then slid down the wall. He let out a sigh as he sank into the water's chilly embrace, not bothering to try to cover himself.

The dark hair on his chest continued in a trail that led to the thicker triangle around his dick. The water was freezing. Wasn't that all supposed to *shrink* in the cold?

Wow...

Not lusting after him was going to be a hell of a lot harder than she thought.

Chapter Two

"What's your name?" the Earthling said.

She was hovering over him, staring at him with eyes as blue as Neptune. They weren't as small as most humans'. Her face was oval—a bit like his own kind. It was strangely pleasant to look at, even surrounded by all that yellow-gold hair. Still, he wanted her to leave so he could deal with his humiliation privately.

"Zemanni."

"Cool." She cleared her throat. "I mean, are you cool enough? Should I get some ice?"

"More cold water."

"I guess they don't have manners on your planet," she mumbled, turning up the water to make the level rise. She took off her coat and tossed it into the hallway.

The water was heating quickly from the energy he was putting off. The parts of his body that were submerged felt better. He slid beneath the surface and let out a sigh. Through the water, he could hear the Earthling make a bothersome noise.

He remembered the form of a being with gills, and tried

to modify his body so that he could siphon enough oxygen from the water to tell her to shut up. It was more out of habit than anything else, but his idiotic human body interpreted the thought as him wanting to breathe, even though he was submerged. Water rushed into his lungs.

How could it burn? It was *water*.

His body reacted with instincts encoded in the DNA he'd stolen from Eric Peterson—the man whose form Zemanni was trapped in. Between that, and the Earthling's frantic attempts to pull him out of the water, he managed to sit up.

Water sprayed from his mouth and nose. He felt more burning deep in his chest. His body expelled it with coughs that wracked his body, further tiring him.

The Earthling pounded on his back, and kept repeating, "Are you okay?"

He glared at her as he sucked in breath after breath into his nearly functionless human lungs. He wondered how the species survived with only *two* when they were so inefficient.

Though he'd been assigned to Earth for months, he'd never stayed human this long. And without enough of the quicksilver that usually coursed through his natural form—allowing him to alter his shape at will—he couldn't change even the simplest thing about himself.

He could feel his cells stabilizing based on the only DNA pattern they had available to them—*human* DNA.

"Are. You. Okay." The woman was gripping his shoulders tightly, shaking him.

"Stop that," he shouted.

"I'm not going to let you drown yourself in my tub."

"I didn't know I was going to drown."

"How could you…" Her voice trailed off and she shook her head. "Earthlings need to breathe air." She said the words loudly and with crisp enunciation, as if she thought he needed help to understand her.

"I know that."

"So you *were* trying to drown yourself?"

"No, I… I just forgot for a moment."

Forgot his two pathetic lungs. The single pounding organ that pumped the thin, runny blood through his human veins. His barely functional eyes and all of the hair, hair, *hair* everywhere, all over his body.

He grabbed a fistful of the stuff on top of his head and tugged on it, wishing he could pull off this weirdly sensitive skin. But then he couldn't grow back another. He'd used almost every drop of quicksilver he had left in his system to piece himself back together after that Lyrian female had torn him to pieces.

"Stop." The Earthling leaned forward, wrapping her arms around him.

At least *this* female only had two arms. And she didn't seem like she was trying to kill him.

"Calm down," she said. "I'm going to help you, if I

can."

Her embrace felt good. Comforting in a way that disgusted him. He shouldn't need to be comforted. At the same time, the fact that she was offering... It made his chest feel tight, his internal pump—heart—suffused with strange energy.

There was a rich and powerful scent on her that flooded his awareness with her proximity.

"You smell delicious." He wasn't sure why he spoke the words out loud, unless it was from the sudden *want* surrounding the smell that flooded his senses.

His brain was different, too. His mouth, his speech centers. This stabilizing form was pushing all that he was familiar with about himself away and replacing it with feelings that were alien. *Alien.*

What a ridiculous species.

She jerked back from him, stumbling away until she hit the counter behind her. "You said you wouldn't try to eat me."

"What? No." He shook his head, leaning heavily on his thighs. Hairy thighs. "Something on your clothing smells appealing."

She sniffed her shirt experimentally. "All I smell is coffee."

He'd smelled coffee before. But only when he was borrowing an Earthling's form. Being trapped in this form was altering his perceptions to a troubling degree.

Vapor pits, he was becoming a human. He might be stuck this way forever.

His ship was destroyed, his supplies gone. He could try to negotiate with one of the groups of sentients on Earth that he'd been sent to hunt, offering an exchange of resources for the use of their communication systems. But if he managed to send a signal requesting help, his reputation would be ruined.

The greatest assassin in the galaxy, taken down by a pair of Lyrians who'd adopted an Earthling, of all things.

He'd known he was off his game. He had been ever since he'd taken on the DNA of Eric Peterson. Something in the Earthling's genetic makeup had troubled Zemanni since the moment he'd sampled it. Strange impulses and distracting thoughts he couldn't explain.

He'd never questioned what he did before. Never wanted more than to be the best at taking out targets and gathering power.

Now, he wanted… Zemanni didn't understand what.

"Do you want some coffee?"

"What?"

"Coffee." She arched an eyebrow at him when he just stared at her. "Hello? What we were just talking about? It's an Earth beverage that many of us enjoy."

"I know what coffee is."

"Oh my God. Did you use your shapeshifting abilities to become a giant asshole, or is that part of your natural form?"

He glared at her. She met his gaze and held it. It wasn't something he was used to.

More strange stimulation coursed through his body— this time, primarily affecting his skin. It tingled, especially in his hands. His groin was also starting to feel…tight.

"Do you want some or not?" she said.

He needed to get more fluid into this form. With all the quicksilver he'd lost, he felt desiccated.

"Yes."

She turned toward the door, but stopped suddenly. "If I leave, are you going to try to drown again?"

"I wasn't trying to drown in the first place."

"Right."

She reached for one of the silver handles above the bathtub and turned it. Cold water started spraying from a nozzle high above, like rain. The droplets stung where they struck his flesh, but the cold was soothing. She reached into the tub and pulled out a stopper that was keeping the now-warm water in place.

She smirked at him and said, "Just in case."

As soon as she'd left the room, he muttered, "Infuriating Earthling."

He didn't even know her name yet.

Why should he care? He'd be gone as soon as he could manage it. Though being able to call her by name might be helpful while he was in her care.

He shivered. Help and care. Help and care. Words that came to his consciousness with increasing frequency.

"Eric Peterson." He spat out the words. "Of all the DNA templates to be stuck with, why yours?" Zemanni struck the water in front of him, sending it splashing up along the tile.

He heard the woman's voice from another room. "Everything okay in there?"

"I'm not drowning," he shouted back. His lungs still burned, but yelling released some of the energy coiling inside of him. The emotional energy, anyway.

The other—the quicksilver—was starting to fade as well, what little he had in reserve going dormant.

"What's your name?" he called out.

"Brooke. And if we keep shouting like this, someone's going to call the cops. Not all of my neighbors are at work."

He let himself fall silent. Knowing her name soothed him for some reason. But the very fact that it did agitated him once more.

How the hell was he going to get out of this one?

Cygnus X, he was even starting to *think* like an Earthling. His people had no notion of hell—or heaven. There was only each commission—gaining rank, and watching his back as he tried to get in position behind other people's to strike when they least expected it.

A shiver passed over him. If a rival Scorpiian found him like this, unbelievably vulnerable, he was fairly sure what they would do. His kind had no pity, but they did have what Earthlings might call a mean streak accompanying their avarice.

Zemanni had resources that many would envy. Resources that could only be accessed by a shapeshifting Scorpiian. Of course, if they didn't use the right codes, they'd be in for a most unpleasant surprise.

He was thinking in circles. He needed to focus. Heal. Replenish himself. Then come up with a plan.

His tissues were settling into his new form, the high temperature of his body subsiding thanks to the Earthling's help. It didn't take concentration to make his form stay together anymore. The glow from the quicksilver seams had dimmed, leaving behind small lines of white scar tissue.

He had delved deeper into his shapeshifting abilities than any other Scorpiian he'd ever heard of. He would test the limits of how much of himself he could change internally. As long as he had quicksilver in his system— even dormant—he'd always been able to change back.

But most of his quicksilver had poured from his body during the Lyrian's attack. His emergency supply had been on his ship, which was now utterly destroyed.

Being human would be challenging, but he knew he would be able to adapt to the needs of this new form as they arose. Food. Sleep. Air. Eliminations.

A disgusted grunt escaped him—a low booming sound

from this ridiculously huge chest cavity. Even his thoughts sounded like the specific human whose form he had taken. That wasn't supposed to happen.

He thought through his options. There were several alien factions operating on Earth. Approaching them would be too dangerous. But there were also humans who had made contact and were smart enough to be discreet about it.

One in particular might be of use to him. Dr. Carol Addison. His exhaustive research on the planet revealed that she had traded goods for enough technology to set up an advanced genetics lab. But how would he even get to her?

It was another problem for another time. First, he needed to secure his base of operations with this human. And adapt to his new form.

Zemanni took a deep breath to check and see how well his lungs were functioning now. The smell—the *amazing* smell—was stronger.

He sniffed the air like an animal—and barely managed to care. What he'd smelled on the woman was a pale shadow of this.

He stood and stepped out of the tub. The floor was cool and slippery against his feet. He carefully made his way out of the room. There was carpet in the hall, and the absorbent material made keeping his footing much easier.

The smell grew stronger as he turned a corner and saw the Earthling standing with her back to him, humming a song. The woman who was helping him.

Brooke.

Another strange pang filled his chest. He rubbed at the muscles, trying to make the feeling go away. The motion made the hairs on his skin pull, annoying him.

The aroma of the dark liquid she was brewing somehow promised healing and contentment. His mind felt more alert already.

Humans talked about the stimulating effects of coffee. It was supposed to make their brains function better. And it smelled delicious.

If he was going to be trapped in this appallingly sensitive form, he might was well enjoy it. He reached for the glass container of the liquid.

Brooke turned, her eyes widening as she saw him. Her gaze slid down his body, then snapped back to his face. He wondered if she was as disgusted as he was by all of his borrowed form's hair and bulk. Assessing her body for reactions, he noted that her pupils were dilated and her nipples had stiffened beneath her shirt, which was still damp from helping him in the bathtub.

"What are you doing?" she said.

"I need to drink."

She looked back at the coffee, then stepped forward to intercept him. She went so far as to put a hand on his chest.

His breath caught and his heart rate increased. A wave of extremely pleasant sensation sizzled over all of his skin.

While the stimulus was strong around where she touched him, it was actually most intense in the bizarre reproductive organ at the bottom of his torso.

Strange.

He looked at her hand on his chest, then back to her face. Did she actually think she could stop him? She would not think so for long.

Chapter Three

She was touching an alien. A *naked* alien.

Sure, she'd already pretty much draped his body over hers while helping him in from the car. And she'd had her arms around him while pulling him out of the tub. But this was different.

His skin was still hot, but didn't feel feverish like it had earlier. He was dripping wet from the bath, his dark hair plastered in jagged little hooks around his forehead. The glowing silver lines had faded into what looked like totally badass scars all over his body.

So much muscle. So much strength. He radiated masculine energy. Her fingers twitched as she fought the urge to slide her hand through his chest hair.

Zemanni grabbed her wrist and pulled her hand away. Had she offended him somehow? Maybe he wasn't okay with her touching him.

She was about to apologize, but he grabbed her other wrist and pushed her back against the fridge, drawing her arms up over her head. He pinned her against the cold surface with his body so that she couldn't move.

Oh, damn. Was she in *that* kind of movie? Because with this guy, she was down with that.

He shifted his grip so that he could hold her wrists with one huge, strong hand. Now that the other was free, he could use it to unbutton her jeans. Maybe slide it up under her shirt.

He reached for the coffee pot.

"Seriously?" she said. "You can't drink that yet. It's too hot."

He let out a grunt, stretching to try to reach it as she squirmed in his grasp.

This was the bathtub all over again. She strained against his grip, but couldn't budge him. It wasn't nearly as sexy with him about to hurt himself. Again.

"Listen to me, Zemanni. You just nearly drowned yourself. You obviously have no idea how human bodies work."

"Yes, I do." His voice was a low rumble.

"No, you don't." She managed to get one of her hands free and immediately used it to latch on to his arm and pull it away from the counter. "That coffee will burn you. Like damaging burns. If you can just wait a minute."

"I need liquid."

"Then I'll get you some water."

"My body has cooled."

"That's not what… Oh my God, you're impossible."

"No, *you* are the one who's impossible. You Earthlings

with all of your differentiated nerve endings and tactile sensitivities."

"What does that even mean?"

He shoved himself back against her, pressing his entire body to hers as he recaptured her wrist and pinned it next to the other above her head. Her breath caught in her throat. Part of her knew that she should be afraid. But she wasn't.

She could tell he wasn't trying to force himself on her. Hell, if she thought he was interested, she'd be all over him in an instant. And she truly didn't think he wanted to hurt her.

Himself she wasn't so sure about yet.

He pushed harder, bringing more of their bodies into contact. "How do you even breathe with these solid air bladders? And almost all of your organs have discreet functions, with no backups."

"We get by," she said.

"You have no idea how precarious your existence is. How limited."

Now he was just pissing her off.

"Actually, I'm the one who understands my 'human limits'," she said. "You're the one who tried to breathe water and wants to drink scalding hot coffee straight from the pot. Human bodies can't do those things, and I'm okay with it. There's plenty that's awesome about being human."

"Like what?"

His face was inches from hers, his breath warm on her

face. He was staring at her intently, like he was daring her to prove to him that being a human was a worthwhile experience. She decided to go for it.

She kissed him.

All of his muscles locked up. She could feel it. She could also feel the softness and warmth of his lips. He didn't pull away.

She moved her mouth against his, urging him to kiss her back. His grip on her wrists loosened. It was a good start.

With her hands free, she wrapped one arm around his shoulders to hold herself tight against him and used the other to bury her fingers in his hair. She gently raked her nails along his scalp before grabbing a fistful of the dark strands to guide his head to tilt slightly to the side.

She kept working his mouth, trying to get him to open to her, to kiss her back, to do *anything* but just stand there pinning her to her fridge. His hands dropped to her hips.

Better.

Running her tongue along the seam of his lips, she ran her nails over his scalp again. He groaned, giving her the opening she needed. She slipped her tongue deeper, until it met his, caressing it with long strokes.

She really hoped he wouldn't accidentally bite her. Or on-purpose bite her. He might have sensed her doubts, because he shifted his hands to her ass, pulling her hips firmly against his.

A shower *and* a grower. Damn. She was going to make

this happen.

She released his mouth, pulling his hair firmly to the side to give her better access to his neck and ear. His hands clenched her tight as she nipped and kissed his neck.

Pulling herself up higher on his shoulders, she sucked his earlobe into her mouth, tonguing it, running her teeth over it. He moaned, rocking his hips against her and tugging at her jeans—which weren't the best wardrobe choice now that she thought about what they were doing. The fabric had to be chafing him.

She managed to tear herself away from the lust clouding her mind, and said, "You're going to hurt yourself."

"I don't give a rank about the coffee anymore."

Give a rank? She'd ask about it later.

"That's not what I mean. You're going to hurt your dick on my jeans."

"My what?" He was still grinding against her.

Why hadn't she worn a skirt to work? Oh right, because it was freezing outside. The heat they were generating made it feel like summer in her kitchen.

"I want your mouth on me again," he said.

It wasn't a sweet nothing whispered in her ear or even a polite request. His tone was commanding in a way she'd never experienced. Sure, she'd dated guys who tried to act macho in the bedroom, but Zemanni... There was an intensity about him that made his confidence completely irresistible.

She'd dated a string of broken men before. This took it to a whole new level.

Rescuer and now this. Brooke wasn't even sure how to classify it. She had better things to think about anyway.

"Now," he said, thrusting against her again and wincing, even as he pulled her hips tighter against his.

She smirked at him. "You asked for it."

Chapter Four

What was she planning? Zemanni had lived far too long to not know when someone was plotting against him. But she was also pressing herself against him, and stars help him, he couldn't get enough of it.

He'd never had cause to kiss someone during an assignment. And if he had, he doubted it would have felt like this while he was only disguised as a human. Beneath his skin, he'd always been a Scorpiian.

The solid flesh that had felt like a prison was beginning to feel like…an opportunity. His heart beat, sending his thin human blood coursing through veins that seemed to swell in anticipation.

His "dick", as she'd called it, had actually grown, the sensation oddly reminiscent of shifting in his natural form. It was no longer soft, but incredibly hard. The skin had been pulled tight, bringing all of the nerve endings within the organ to full alert. He couldn't believe how much he could sense through it.

There was warmth at the apex of her legs. Warmth and wetness. He felt drawn to that heat, driving his dick against her, *seeking.*

Her clothing was a mix of soft fabric and hard seams. Not what he wanted.

He wanted softness and…something he couldn't name.

"Step back," she said.

"No."

She let out a frustrated sound, but then arched an eyebrow and smirked at him. Leaning forward again, she bit his neck in the tantalizing way she'd been doing earlier. His dick throbbed, *need* coursing through him along with his human blood.

Pulling his earlobe into her mouth, she sucked it, ran her tongue around it, and again caught it between her teeth with just enough pressure to resonate through his body. She released it, then blew on the wet surface, making his skin respond in yet another way.

More stimulation. More pleasure. That was what he wanted.

"I promise I'll make it worthwhile for you," she whispered.

Such a promise. For a moment, it was as though she was speaking his language. Offering an exchange—usually services for resources. But she couldn't know how those words would affect a Scorpiian.

What was she offering? More of this? More *than* this?

And what could he offer in return?

She pushed on his chest, and he let her move him back a

pace. If her offering wasn't sufficient, he wanted to be able to press her against the surface behind her again and resume their earlier activity. The pleasure it gave him was worth the moments of pain.

She raked her nails through the hair covering his chest. A thrum of pleasure jolted along his nerves. The hairs caught against her fingers, heightening the sensation. Perhaps it had a use after all.

Brooke seemed to enjoy looking at it, at least. And touching it. Her fingertips trailed down the line of dark hair, along the ripples of muscles covering his abdomen.

"You want my mouth on you again?" she said.

"Yes." Hadn't she understood him earlier?

"What about my hands?"

Those, too, but he was more interested in—

His thoughts cut out abruptly at the overload of pleasure that hit his brain as she wrapped her hand around his dick. He half-fell, half-leaned forward, catching himself with his hands on the cold metal of the fridge behind her.

Her face was just next to his ear again, and she brushed it with her cheek. She tightened her grip, pulling the flesh of his dick in a long, slow stroke.

"Stars," he grunted out, thrusting against her hand.

What is *this?*

While she kept up her stroking, she went after his ear and neck again, stimulating them with her mouth. So many parts of his body were giving him input that he wanted to pay attention to all at once.

So much sensation. So much pleasure.

It was impossible to track it all. He was tempted to just give himself over to the experience, but that would require allowing himself to be distracted to a degree that he had never allowed before.

And yet…he thought it might be worth it.

She took mercy on the pleasure centers of his brain, ending the kisses and bites along his neck and ear. He missed it.

"More," he said. "I want more."

The look in her eyes disturbed him. He'd never seen that particular form of confidence. She knew what she was doing to him—and was enjoying it. As a Scorpiian, he would have found it an affront. But as a human…

He enjoyed that she was enjoying herself as well—that they were *sharing* this. He wondered if her body was sending her signals at all similar to what he felt, and if not, what he would need to do to provoke them.

"You said you wanted my mouth on you," she said.

She'd just *had* her mouth on him. What was she talking about now?

With that same smirk on her face, she slipped down between his arms, landing softly on her knees. He was about to ask what she was doing, but decided against it. She still had one hand on his dick, lightly brushing the backs of her fingers along its length. Each stroke sent another thrum of pleasure through him.

She was also trailing her fingertips along his thigh. The hairs on his skin again enhanced the sensation—especially when she used her nails. Her lips were so close to where her hands were working, and she had alluded to putting her mouth on him again.

He wondered what it would be like to feel the soft flesh of her lips on his dick, the warm wetness of her mouth. Did humans even do such a thing?

The Coalition had sent him to track down and assassinate rogue aliens operating on Earth without the High Council's approval—and thus without them receiving any benefits. He'd only studied Earthlings enough to fit in while hunting his targets.

He wished that he knew more about their mating protocols. This was part of it—he at least knew that much. But there were so many questions he didn't even know how to formulate.

Instead of trying to ask, he said, "I don't see your mouth on me yet."

"I hope you're not always this impatient."

He gripped the sides of the fridge's door, waiting to see what she would do next, how his body would react. What she was doing with her hand was more relaxing than anything else. Yet at the same time, he could feel it building a tightly coiled energy within him. A gentle stimulus that—

She turned her face toward his dick, holding it still as

she darted her tongue along its length. He let out another grunt, his eyes rolling shut as his hands tightened on the metal door.

That was apparently only the beginning. He felt her lips on the tip of his dick, wrapping around it, taking him into her mouth. Her tongue pressed against the underside of his length, flicking it, swirling around. She sucked on him, as she'd done his ear and his tongue, but feeling it here was profoundly...*more.*

He was making himself vulnerable to her. She could bite him, and a wound there would be extremely painful. But she'd only been helpful—so incredibly helpful—so far.

She wouldn't hurt him. That realization alone made his chest feel almost painfully tight yet again. He was a fool. He *trusted* her.

It was hard not to, under the circumstances. He forced his eyes open so that he could watch her work her magic on him.

In and out, she moved his dick around her mouth, her lips, her face. She gripped the rest of his length with both hands, guiding it where she wanted. She ran her tongue up in a long stroke along the bottom, all the way to the tip, before taking him deep in her mouth again.

Stars, the pleasure.

It coursed through him, consumed him, set every cell on fire in a way that was infinitely more enjoyable than his acclimation had been. It almost—*almost*—made the pain worth it. This experience of physical sensation was unlike anything he'd ever known.

His hips started to thrust against her without his conscious intent, a deep instinct rising up through the human DNA that had taken over his existence. The lines of scarring where he had reassembled himself began to glow, matching the sensation in his solid flesh.

She increased the strength of her grip, tightened her lips around him, quickened her tongue. Her mouth pumped along his length, sucking and licking. His dick throbbed with increasing urgency that echoed through his form. A pressure was building inside of him that felt as though it could break him apart, yet he couldn't bring himself to care.

All he cared about was this moment, this ecstasy, feeling her mouth on him, the tightness of her hands and lips, the constant movement of her tongue and—

"Stars!"

A brief flash of silver light blinded him for a moment, leaving an afterimage burned against his retinas. His body felt electrified, like the apex of a change, but so much stronger. The throbbing in his dick turned into a pounding pulse, each beat sending arcs of pleasure ripping through his body with an intensity that made his knees start to buckle.

As the feeling began to fade, she released him and sat back on her heels. Zemanni staggered back till he hit the wall, then slid to the ground.

His breathing was fast, his heartbeat faster. His body was filled with a feeling of *life* that made all of his other experiences pale in comparison. And his dick just kept tingling, even as it subsided to its original form.

He gasped for breath, finally managing to ask, "What was that?"

Brooke shrugged, then smiled at him.

"Perks of being human."

Chapter Five

Brooke knew she was good. She hadn't realized she was *that* good. But she could tell when she'd rocked someone's world. Zemanni's had definitely been tilted on its axis. He looked kind of shaken, actually.

"Are you okay?" she said.

He shook his head, swallowing hard enough that she could watch his throat work. "No."

Dread knotted her stomach at the thought. He seemed human, and had talked about being trapped in this form. He'd even complained about his human anatomy. Was there something different about him that would make sex harmful?

"I didn't hurt you, did I?"

"No," he said. "I want more."

Oh. Not so different at all, then.

She let out a shaky laugh as she stood. "Yeah, yeah. That's what they all say."

The coffee was still too hot for him to drink, so she grabbed some ice cubes from the freezer and plunked them into the mug she'd set out for him. She watched the ice melt as she poured the dark drink over them. Just to be safe, she took out a spoon and stirred everything, making sure there were no ice chunks he might choke on.

When it was ready, she turned to him with the mug in hand. He was still sitting with his back against the wall, watching her every move with that intense stare of his.

"Here." She handed him the drink.

No "thank you", no smile. He didn't even acknowledge it with a nod. He just threw his head back, chugging the entire contents of the mug.

"Maybe slow down a little?" she said.

He shivered. It was no wonder, with him sitting on the cold floor still soaking wet. But then his scars started to glow lightly—pulsing, almost like they were keeping time with his heartbeat. If he had a heart.

He leaned his head back against the wall, dropping his hand and the mug onto his lap. His eyes were closed, and he let out a sigh as some of the lines of tension faded from around his eyes.

Behold the miracle of coffee...

"So, you really are trapped in this form?" she said.

The look of ease vanished as his eyes opened and he fixed her with that predatory stare. "Why do you ask?"

"I'm just trying to get my bearings here. Figure out what's going on."

"It's best if you don't."

"Really?" She plucked the mug from his grasp, then

turned back to the coffee pot and began making him an exact duplicate of the first drink. Once she had finished it, she turned and handed the mug back to him, then said, "I think I need to know at least a few things."

"Such as?"

Dozens of questions started lining up in her mind. Was Earth being invaded? Were there more like him out there? What had ripped him apart and why?

She doubted she'd get straight answers to any of those questions. Instead, she stuck with the more immediate concern.

"You said your body is human."

"Yeah."

"How do I put this delicately?" She realized she probably didn't *need* to, since he was an alien and all. "Why didn't anything come out of your dick when I blew you?"

The furrows between his eyebrows deepened and his lip curled up. "Something's supposed to come out of it?"

She busted out laughing, but stopped just as suddenly. "Oh God. Please tell me I'm not going to have to teach you how to go to the bathroom."

"Why would you have to do that?" He lifted his finger and pointed to the archway that led to the kitchen. "It's around the corner."

"Oh no. Okay, you know what? That's what the Internet is for." As long as she was very, very careful in her search.

She shook her head, hoping they wouldn't have to deal with that particular aspect of humanity until later. As he took a slower sip of his coffee, his scars glowed again. Maybe it wouldn't be an issue after all.

"The way your skin glows, you can't be completely human," she said.

"I'm not."

"You're a Scorpiian."

He drained his mug, then handed it to her. "More."

"Are you sure you should be drinking this much caffeine?" She started working on his third cup. "I mean, who knows what it'll really do to your system."

"This liquid is highly compatible with my biology. And I need to replenish my fluids."

Maybe that was why there hadn't been "the usual contribution" when she'd blown him. It had thrown her off her game a little, to sense all the other signals of an orgasm without that very important one. It also opened up a whole slew of possibilities, if he lacked that complication that most human bodies came with.

Came. She snickered to herself.

"Something is amusing you?" he said.

"It…isn't something I want to explain." She handed him the third cup, then squatted across from him, leaning against the cabinets near the floor. "A real human would probably be getting jittery right now. Caffeine is a stimulant."

"I can feel that. It's boosting my remaining quicksilver."

"Quicksilver?"

"A vital fluid among my kind."

"Let me guess. It enables you to change your form."

He paused with the mug halfway to his lips. Very nice lips. That would be giving her very nice thoughts if it wasn't for the serious pair of murder eyes he was leveling at her.

She held up her hands and shook her head. "Lucky guess, that's all. I watch a lot of movies and read a lot of books. You keep talking about being trapped in a human form. That kind of implies you can turn into other ones. There has to be something about your anatomy that helps with that."

Slowly, he lifted the mug again and drank. He kept his gaze trained on her, though. When he'd emptied it, he handed it back to her.

"You're welcome," she said.

She rose, turning toward the counter. Another amusing thought occurred to her—one she *could* share.

"I just realized, you're literally replacing your blood with coffee," she said.

"No, I'm not. I have human blood in my veins now."

She let out a little snort. "It loses something if I say, 'You're replacing your alien blood with coffee'."

"The coffee is only boosting the functionality of my quicksilver."

"Barrel of laughs, this one," she murmured.

Zemanni just stared at her. Damn, that was a cool name. She pointed to the empty coffee pot. "You want more?"

"No."

"Suit yourself." She shrugged, then crossed the room to the sink.

As she rinsed out the cup, she felt the hairs on the back of her neck stand on end. She turned off the water, but kept the mug in her hand. Her skin felt like there was an electrical current next to her. She'd felt something similar once, when she'd been standing too close to a frayed wire.

What if she was wrong about him? What if he wasn't a friendly alien visitor in need of help? He could just be using her.

Right, using me for coffee and a blowjob. And a cold bath that nearly drowned him.

Out of the corner of her eye, she saw that he wasn't sitting on the floor anymore, and she hadn't heard him move. She wasn't sure where he was. Her heart began to thud as her brain went into overdrive, inventing nightmare scenarios one after another.

He touched her shoulder and she wheeled around with the mug raised defensively. He caught her wrist again, stopping her arm. Then he grabbed her by the back of her neck. The back, not the front. That was reassuring at least.

His gaze was still predatory, but the coldness had left it. The look he cast on her was all fire.

"What do you want?" she whispered.

"More."

"More coffee?"

He lowered her arm so that the mug rested on the counter, then said, "No."

Chapter Six

There was more to explore in this human form. Much more. Zemanni had had a taste, when Brooke had used her mouth on him. His changing instincts told him that was only the beginning.

He would have this woman. As soon as he figured out how.

"Let me guess," she said. "You want my mouth on you again?"

Her voice held a note of tension that he hadn't detected before. It was almost as if she was afraid of him.

Not long ago, he wouldn't have cared. But in this form, the thought sent a wave of prickling heat through him— almost a form of pain. He didn't want her to fear him.

She licked her lips, and the energy of the unfamiliar emotion shifted. He wanted to pleasure her, *needed* to.

He pulled her against his chest, pressing his lips against hers as she'd done to him earlier. She had used his hair to guide him, so he released her neck and ran his fingers through the unbelievably soft sun-gold waves. His fingers clenched around a lock of it, holding enough to not hurt her as he urged her head to tilt.

His nails were too short to stimulate her skin as she had done to him, but she still let out a moan, giving him his first opportunity to strike. As her lips parted, he drove his tongue into her mouth. She wrapped her arms around his neck, pulling herself up along his body. With their heads at a more even level, he could begin his conquest in earnest.

His tongue tangled with hers, demanding reciprocation. He only relented when he noticed her breath starting to catch, small gasps interrupting their sparring.

The next target was to the side. He had been nearly overcome the first time she'd run her teeth along his earlobe. The attentions she had given to his body displayed a level of expertise he strove to match.

He had seen her look of confidence—of *victory*—in knowing how her actions were affecting him. He wanted to experience that thrill as well.

Releasing her mouth, he kissed the skin along her jaw. He didn't want to allow her a moment's reprieve from the pleasure he was giving her. At the same time, he didn't rush his movements. Her brain would need time to process the signals her nerve endings were sending.

He reached her neck, raking his teeth over her skin— being careful not to apply too much pressure. She let out a low moan that resounded through his body. His dick twitched—a movement he hadn't known it was capable of.

With her clinging to him, he had more freedom of

movement while they stayed in contact. He released her hair, bringing both hands to her buttocks and pressing her hips against his hard member as he sucked on the side of her neck.

She groaned again, grinding her hips against him. The fabric of her jeans was still uncomfortable. It needed to be removed. All of her clothing did.

Moons, he would have to stop kissing her to deal with that. Preferably for the least amount of time possible.

He reached between them and unfastened her jeans. She had already removed her boots and socks—probably when she went to the kitchen. That would facilitate his work.

Releasing her neck took a surprising amount of willpower. Allowing any space between them did. He felt almost magnetized to her. He wanted their bodies to interlock again, as they had when she took him into her mouth. No—in a different way. He hadn't quite figured it out yet. But it was only a matter of time.

He dropped to his knees, pulling her jeans and panties with him and helping her step out of them. As he did, she practically tore her shirt from her body, tossing it across the room. She reached behind her back to release the elastic material of her undergarment and threw it from her as well.

From where he was squatting, he had a close view of her external reproductive structure. Burnished gold hair in a triangle at the apex of her legs. And the air close to her skin was filled with the most incredible smell—heady and sweet.

He had no idea how humans went about this, but he didn't care to stop to ask. The instincts in this body were strong. Zemanni would follow them. He grabbed her hips, and pressed his mouth to her with the same fervor as he'd shown her neck.

Remembering how she had used her tongue on his dick, he slid his tongue between the folds of her flesh. She gasped, grabbing fistfuls of his hair as his tongue passed over a nub of slightly firmer tissue that seemed sensitive, judging from her response to the contact. Perhaps it was some sort of sensory nexus or nerve cluster?

He returned to the spot, circling it and flicking it. As her grip on his hair increased, so did his attentions. The muscles of her thighs tightened as her breath rate increased. The reaction seemed reflexive, but made access more difficult.

With a grunt, he wrapped his arms around her hips, then lifted her from her feet and set her back down on the counter. Their gazes locked for a brief moment. Her eyes were wide and her parted lips swollen as she dragged breath into her body.

His actions were producing the desired result. He still wanted more.

He pushed her legs wide, assessing her anatomy, calculating how they would best fit together, processing everything that he'd experienced with her so far and what he knew from all the human DNA he'd assimilated. With renewed determination, he put his lips to the nexus of stimulation, sucking it as she had done to him.

She reached out to hold on to the side of her fridge and the edge of a cabinet that stuck out past the counter, her eyes closed. There was so much wetness and heat issuing from inside her. Her slit was slick with wanting. He was understanding more and more.

He pressed his fingers to her.

"Zemanni..." She draped her legs over his shoulders, shifting her hips to give him better access.

He pinched her sensory nexus between his lips as he slid his fingers deep. Her central core flexed around them, squeezing them tight. The musculature of this part of her reproductive anatomy was fascinating.

Remembering how his own body had thrust against her without him even consciously telling it to do so, he started sliding his fingers in and out, swirling her nexus with his tongue.

"Oh, God," she gasped. "How do you know how to do this?"

Instinct.

The same instinct that told him to stand and drive his dick into her, to thrust himself in her core over and over again until that same explosion of energy flooded both of their bodies. But she'd already done that for him once.

He didn't like unbalanced scales.

Her grip tightened on his hair and he increased his pace, the intensity of his mouth on her. He sucked and pulled, alternating the stimuli to try to bring her the greatest pleasure.

He felt her body tense, then her feet dug into his back as her spine arched, lifting most of her body completely off the counter for a moment. The muscles around his fingers pulsed harder and faster.

When his own body had peaked in its pleasure threshold, she had increased her pace. He did the same for her, moving his hand more quickly, his tongue more firmly. She cried out, thrashing on the counter as she bucked her hips against him.

His body responded. His dick throbbed and his entire pelvic region felt tight and heavy. He wanted to feel the full effect of this aspect of human physicality.

And now, the score was even.

Chapter Seven

Stars were flickering in Brooke's eyes as Zemanni pulled his fingers from her. She opened her mouth to speak, but he stood so quickly, she didn't have a chance to say anything.

He grabbed the back of her neck again, pulling her face to his for another soul-searing kiss. His tongue invaded her mouth, conquered it. And that wasn't enough.

She felt his dick at the entrance of her core for a brief second before he drove himself into her. Again, he didn't give her time to catch her breath. He immediately started thrusting into her, fast and hard. His dick was so big, she couldn't believe she was managing him.

On the heels of the incredible climax he'd already given her, her body lit up with a heat that consumed all thought. He stretched her, filled her, compelled her body to give itself to the pleasure that he was pouring into her.

She wrapped her legs around his waist, using them to draw him deeper. He grunted his approval, pulling her closer by wrapping his free arm around her back.

Finally releasing her mouth, he dropped his head, staring

at where they were connected, watching as he pounded into her. She couldn't stop looking at him—the gorgeous alien setting her nerves on fire.

He brought his gaze back to hers, and the wonder that she saw there made her breath catch in her throat. A thrill of something more than physical pleasure poured along her nerve endings along with the resonating thrums of his near-frantic strokes.

Maybe he noticed her reaction, because his expression shuttered. He dropped both hands to her ass, lifting her from the counter and turning them around, then staggering a few paces to the wall and pinning her against it.

Without the counter supporting her weight, she slid farther down his shaft. She tightened her legs around his waist, using her arms on his shoulders to rock against him, meeting his thrusts and grinding her clit against him each time he landed.

Damn, she could let him fuck her like this forever.

Her body wasn't as patient. Sparks were already starting to sizzle along nerves that had been stimulated past anything she'd thought she could take. The first orgasm had primed her system—like a warm up before the main event, and her senses were going all out for this one.

He held her with his intense stare, until his eyes widened suddenly, then clenched shut. His fingers dug into her hips, dancing at the edge between pain and pleasure. His dick, already stretching her core as far as it could go, started to pulse, each throb booming through her body like a drum.

The pounding beat pushed her over the edge. Her climax tore through her, hitting her bone-deep. She clawed at his back, hips thrashing against his, lost in sensations that struck at her awareness from everywhere in her body. Her thoroughly kissed lips, her love-bite covered neck, and most intensely, where his dick was still jack-hammering into her.

"Stars." His voice rose as he said again, "Stars."

He pinned her to the wall, his dick buried to the hilt, each pulse of his shaft amplifying the booming aftershocks of her own orgasm. All she could do was try to breathe—to feel his heat soaking into her, the sweat coating their bodies mingling.

His grip on her ass loosened for a moment, but then he tightened his fingers again, kneading her flesh. He angled his hips away from her slowly, but then pushed his softening dick back in deeper.

She'd never had a lover who seemed so reluctant for sex to be over. But Zemanni was keeping their hips pinned together, like he didn't want to slip out of her.

The presence of him inside of her still was the weirdest comfort. Relaxing instead of stimulating.

"Again," he said.

She started to laugh. He sucked in a quick breath, closing his eyes, then blew it out slowly.

"The vibrations you're making..." he said. "I like them."

"I liked the vibrations you made, too. But we're going to have to wait a while before we can do anything like that again."

The furrow between his eyebrows deepened. "How long?"

"I don't know. Every guy is different. But we're going to have to, you know…disengage."

He looked like he was going to argue, but then he stepped away from the wall, letting her unwrap her legs and put her feet back on the ground. Her knees felt more than a little unsteady.

"Maybe we should go sit on the couch," she said. "Do you want any more coffee?"

"Later."

The predatory stare was back, but this time, it sent a shiver of pure delight through her. She could guess exactly what he had in mind. And she had plenty of ideas of her own.

She took his hand and led him to the living room. She didn't have it in her to dress, and with the heat radiating from both of them, she didn't feel the need to wrap up in the blanket that was covering her couch. Instead, they just sat.

She flopped, resting her head on the cushions.

"You had to have done that before," she said. And yet, the raw abandon that he'd shown, the primal urges that he hadn't held back a single bit, made her wonder.

"No."

"Scorpiians don't have sex?"

He paused for a moment, then said, "Not like that."

"How do you do it, then?"

"You don't want to know."

She shrugged. "I'll take your word for it."

The stare was getting a little awkward. They needed something to do to fill the time.

Elliot's game console—actually, *her* console, since she'd bought it, after all—was sitting on the coffee table. Brooke turned it on, along with the TV, then handed Zemanni a controller.

"What's this?" he said.

"A video game."

As the screen came to life, she had a brief moment of misgiving. She turned to Zemanni and poked a finger into his coarse chest hair.

"Don't you dare enjoy this more than sex," she said.

One of his eyebrows arched up, and then... His face transformed. Not in a scary shapeshifting alien kind of way. In a beautiful, eyes crinkling at the corners, lips turning up in a smile, bright teeth flashing, absolutely sincere smile kind of way.

Her heart started to pound. That smile could do a lot of damage. It could put her feet on the slippery slope of starting to fall for him. He let out a deep, booming laugh, and that was even worse. Her toes curled on the thick carpet.

"Don't worry about that," he said. "I can't imagine anything competing with what we did in the kitchen." His expression darkened, but his lips still pulled into a smile. "Except for variations."

Variations?

She swallowed hard, several different "variations" running through her head. The game beeped, giving her an excuse to look away from him.

The sex was incredible. But she needed to do something else with him—something a little more normal than reenacting a porno with a complete stranger. Who was an alien.

"Maybe it *is* that kind of movie," she murmured to herself.

"What kind of movie?"

"Forget it." She shook her head, activating the load screen. "Do you even know what a movie is?"

"Of course. They're very popular on your planet."

She snorted. "*On my planet.* This is so weird."

The game was familiar. It would help take her mind off of the hot alien sitting next to her, and give her a chance to process everything that had happened. Except maybe not. She'd forgotten that the disk in the console was a scifi game.

"Balls," she said.

"What does that mean?"

"It's like a swear. Something we say when we're frustrated. Literally, it means 'testicles'."

He looked down at his crotch for a moment, then back to the screen. "I guess that makes sense. What do you call the cluster of nerves that you most enjoyed me stimulating?"

"You're going to have to narrow that down. You stimulated tons of my 'nerve clusters'."

"The nub in the slit between your legs."

Damn, he was to the point. Then again, he didn't know when not to be. And she kind of liked how direct he was.

"It's called the clitoris," she said.

"Clitoris."

The game finally loaded, saving her from giving him more lessons on Earth names for sexy anatomy. She talked him through the controls briefly as the opening cinematic played.

"It might take you a while to get the hang of it, but try not to stress," she said. "If you die, you respawn."

"Sounds familiar," he murmured.

Was that what had happened to him? Had someone killed him and he… What? Used his shapeshifting abilities to respawn, but now he was stuck in this form?

Zemanni snorted as a spaceship appeared on the backdrop of stars. "That looks almost like a Centaurian vessel. What's it supposed to be?"

"I don't know. This is my ex's game—I never paid attention when he talked about it. I just like shooting things."

Zemanni's smile quirked up on one side. She swore his gaze seemed to soften.

"What?" she said.

"Nothing." He turned to the game as the level started up.

Chapter Eight

One of the opponents Brooke had described appeared on the screen. While Zemanni experimented with the controls, she managed to skillfully dispatch the combatants—some sort of armored humanoids that disintegrated when struck correctly with the right simulated weapon.

Some of the maneuvers she completed were impressive. At least, they would have been in reality.

He watched her fingers on the control, processing how she used the interface to command the figure representing herself in the game. Thoughts of her fingers working on his dick kept intruding on his focus, and it took him longer than he would have expected to grasp the logistics.

As soon as he returned his attention to the screen, he joined her efforts in achieving their objective. Their opponents were dispatched almost as quickly as they appeared. The experience was strangely gratifying.

Sex, coffee, and video games. Perhaps being trapped in a human form wasn't so bad after all.

"Damn, you're a natural at this, too." Brooke smirked at him, casting a quick glance his way before hitting controls in a sequence that disintegrated several opponents.

Sitting with her and playing this game, working toward a shared objective, made that strange warmth return to his chest.

He didn't like it.

Seeking to distract himself from the sensation, he said, "What's an 'ex'?"

"Ugh." Brooke rolled her eyes. "It's someone I used to date. Until he got all weird and super-controlling. You know what dating is, right?"

"Not really."

He had researched Earthlings and their culture more than other Scorpiians might, but only as much as he thought would serve him in navigating their culture while hunting his bounties. The more time he spent with Brooke, the more gaps he found in his knowledge.

She hit another sequence, flanking a group of opponents that he had drawn out into an excellent ambush area on the screen and helping him dispatch them in a pincer movement. He hadn't even had to tell her his plan. It was even more gratifying to work with someone who seemed to think and react like he did.

"When people seem to click—to get along well—we date," she said. "We go out and have fun. Eat, drink, and generally be merry."

"And play video games."

"Sometimes."

"What about sex?"

"Sometimes that, too."

"Your ex—he enjoyed this video game more than sex?"

She snorted. "Yup."

"What an idiot."

She started to laugh, and kept on going long enough that he had to cover her to ensure their opponents didn't disintegrate her representation in the game. The sound of her laughter made that warm tightness surge through his chest again, but this time, it didn't bother him as much.

He was starting to like it.

"Damn, Z," she said. "I could get used to having you around."

That was a good thing, because he had nowhere else to go. The thought chilled the sensation in his chest. He needed to form backup plans immediately.

Returning to his people like this was not an option. Aside from the ridicule he would face, they would see him as weakened and target him. He doubted he would survive long. If another Scorpiian discovered him on Earth trapped in this form, he would face the same fate.

Before determining his options, he had to make peace with his circumstances. He had no supply of quicksilver and no means to access more. His ship had been destroyed.

Even if he could reach a human scientist like Dr. Addison, there was no guaranteeing they would be able to assist him. He needed to integrate his new reality into his fundamental paradigm.

He was stuck like this for the rest of his life.

The only comfort was knowing that he'd already lived longer than most Scorpiians. Spending the next fifty or so decades in a human body was something he could do. Especially if he could spend them like this.

He glanced over at Brooke, watching the intensity she displayed while taking out her opponents in the game. Coffee was intensely enjoyable, both in flavor and the effect on his body. He was sure there were many other experiences that would rival it while he explored the foods he would need to sustain this body.

But nothing could compare to the incredible feeling of his dick buried in her. Everything she'd done to him—and even what he had done to her—had given him pleasure unlike anything he'd ever known.

His dick began to harden at the memories, tingling sensations spreading through him though they weren't even touching. Human bodies were amazing.

He wasn't sure if Brooke would let him stay with her forever, though.

Most Earthlings pair-bonded, much like Sadirians. If he could get her to bond with him, that would facilitate securing this location as a base of operations—and the perks that came along with it.

"You don't have a bondmate, right?" he said.

"No. And I'm up on my shots and don't have any STDs

and I'm on the pill. I'm guessing since you don't 'make a contribution' when we're having sex, that I don't need to worry about getting anything from you, either."

"My form is mostly human, but I'm still fundamentally Scorpiian," he said.

His DNA hadn't *quite* forgotten that, even though the tiny amount of quicksilver remaining in his system had gone dormant. It would be enough to destroy any pathogens that attempted to invade his body, preventing him from passing them on to her.

"Thanks for the reassurance. Excellent job."

He could detect the insincerity of her tone. He shouldn't feel compelled to reassure her, but he did.

"I won't transmit anything to you," he said.

"Cool."

"You don't enjoy video games more than sex, do you?" he asked.

"Of course not. Well, I should say I don't enjoy them as much as sex with *you*. There have been a couple of—"

Before she could finish her statement, he knocked the controller out of her hand, dropping his on the table in front of them. He shoved the table away, giving him more room to maneuver.

"Hey, what are you—"

He swallowed the rest of her question with a kiss, covering her body with his. Her skin was chilled. She must have been growing cold while sitting next to him on the couch naked.

He'd been considering exploring other things they could do with their bodies, but he had to feel himself buried in her again. He wanted to warm her—to *share* his warmth. The emotional desire was as alien to him as the physical ones. He shied away from thinking about how he had been altered at such a profound level and what it meant for his future.

Right now, he wanted to focus on this. Brooke beneath him. Her tongue tangling with his, her passion rising up to crash against his own.

He grabbed her thigh and pulled her legs apart, settling between them. She was still slick, or had become so again. He didn't care which. He just wanted inside of her. Immediately.

Plunging deep, he felt her core wrap around him, muscles tightening. She arced against him, arms sliding around his back and holding him tight. For a moment, he held himself still, taking in the shock and desire on her features.

He ground his pelvis against her clitoris and she gasped. This was different from what they'd done against the wall in the kitchen. He liked this. Their bodies were touching over more of their skin. His heat passed into her, her legs wrapped around his waist.

There wasn't much room on the couch, and the soft cushions were further hampering his movements. He pulled himself from her, and she let out a soft disapproving grunt.

"That was fast," she said.

Did she think he'd already climaxed? He smirked and shook his head, then pulled her from the couch, dragging them both to the floor. The carpet would provide a comfortable location for them. He placed his hand over the apex of her legs, cupping the entire area as he let his fingers press into her slit.

"What is this area called?" Knowing a common vernacular would aid him in pleasuring her.

"Pussy," she gasped, as his thumb circled her clitoris.

He nodded thrusting his fingers into her, deep. She arced off the floor, her hips writhing against his hand. Her breasts shifted in a mesmerizing wavelike pattern. He reached for one, wanting to know if it was as soft as it looked.

As he squeezed it, she gasped again, her eyes rolling shut. Her nipples had stiffened to hard peaks. He ran his thumb over one and she let out a moan. Another sensitive area?

He kept his hand working in her as he bent his head to explore this new opportunity. Pulling her nipple into his mouth, he sucked on it as he had her neck earlier.

"Yes. Z, yes!" She grabbed his hair again, nails dragging across his scalp and sending pinpricks of pleasure along his skin.

No one had called him anything but his name. Hearing her call him 'Z' was yet another special way that they could connect—one that stimulated his chest instead of his groin.

He increased the pressure of his hand on her breast, kneading the soft tissue, circling her nipple with his tongue. When she seemed to start to calm, he shifted to the other side and was met with renewed responses.

There was so much to learn.

His dick was starting to ache again, a dull throb building in his balls. He gave a final pull on her nipple with his mouth, sucking it hard, thrusting with his hand and flicking her clitoris every time it was in range of his thumb. Then he released her and let his body fall on top of hers, only supporting himself enough to give her room to breathe.

He wanted them connected. As much as possible.

Wrapping his arms around her back, he grasped her shoulders to make sure his thrusts wouldn't push her away from him. He knew he'd be landing hard, and wanted her to take it—to take every inch of him. He pressed the tip of his dick to the incredible softness and heat of her core, and slowly pushed himself inside.

Her flesh resisted. He felt his dick stretching her, filling her. Her muscles clenched around him, already so close to the pulsing glory of a climax. He wanted to draw out the experience, and at the same time, he could barely contain his desire to push her over that edge and join her in the ecstatic release these forms could provide.

His pelvis hit hers, his dick bottoming out inside of her. He thought he was as deep as he could go, but she wrapped her legs around his waist again, tilting her hips up to meet his and letting him sink even deeper.

He let out a moan, holding himself still as he willed his body to calm. Nuzzling the side of her neck, he said, "Stars. I could do this forever."

Chapter Nine

"You and me both." Brooke wished she could stay in the haze of lust and pleasure he was keeping around her. But she knew eventually she'd have to return to reality.

She had a job and people who counted on her. She couldn't spend all of her time indulging herself with her alien sex toy, no matter how eager he seemed to keep—

He started to move, and the friction sent sparks through her nervous system that shorted out whatever thoughts she'd been about to have. Something about responsibilities?

Two slow thrusts, and he started to build up speed, that huge dick of his demanding her full attention. She'd never walk straight again after him. And she couldn't care less.

"Dammit, Z. You feel too good."

He chuckled against her neck. "I could say the same about you. And I love it when you call me that."

"What, 'Z'?"

She actually felt a tremor flood through his system. She nipped his ear, and made sure her voice was extra breathy against it as she said, "I can think of some other things to call you."

"Like what?"

"Do you know what a jackhammer is?"

He laughed again. Her stomach did a little flip-flop at the sound.

Zemanni lightening up. Zemanni murmuring against her ear, covering her with his body.

She loved how much he took charge during sex. If he wanted her to move, he moved her. If he wanted to touch her, he touched her. And if he wanted to drive his dick deep into her core, making it feel tight and full and so very, very good, she was down with that, too.

He gripped her shoulders more tightly, his hips shifting back and forth faster and faster. He landed harder each time, pulling away and then pounding in.

Yeah, he definitely knew what a jackhammer was.

The way he was holding on to her, keeping them as close as possible, was threatening to bring her feelings into play, though. She was fully ready to lust after this guy. But to care… She wasn't sure about that yet.

Everything he did was so genuine. Sure, he seemed like he could be an asshole, but who couldn't? He'd treated her well enough so far. But then, she hadn't really pushed him.

"Stop." She spoke so suddenly, she even surprised himself.

Z went still immediately, his dick buried inside her. His eyes were wide and his mouth slightly open as he panted for breath. He licked his lips, and her gaze followed the movement of his tongue. Pushing himself up onto his elbows so less of his weight was on her, he glanced down at her body, then back to her eyes.

"Are you okay?" he said.

Her heart felt like it had fallen through her stomach.

Dammit. I just had to test him, didn't I?

She shook her head. She wasn't okay. With a guy like this, she was in dangerous territory—and she wasn't even thinking about him being an alien.

He was gorgeous, strong, confident. He knew what he wanted and wasn't afraid to go for it, unlike most of the guys she'd dated. They'd been broken on the inside, in need of someone to take care of them, and that had lured her like honey.

Z had been broken on the *outside*, but he was solid steel within. She'd known he would challenge her. He'd been doing so almost nonstop. But she hadn't known if he would be decent to her. Until this moment.

"Am I hurting you?" The furrow between his eyebrows deepened and he started to pull away.

She tightened her legs around his waist, holding him deep. A ripple of pleasure shuddered through him, but he kept himself still, staring at her intently. She had a weird feeling that he could be *hers*, if she wanted him to be.

And she did.

"You're not hurting me," she said. "I just…"

He brushed her hair back from her face in a remarkably

gentle movement. Tenderness and passion. Damn, she was in trouble.

"I need you to guide me through this," he said. "I don't know what's going on."

"Neither do I. That's the problem." She let out a sigh. "How long are you going to be here?"

His expression shuttered and he looked away.

"I mean, if this is a pit stop for you, and I'm just a diversion, I need to know not to get attached," she said.

He looked back at her, his eyes widening. The look on his face was the closest thing to sincerity she'd seen from him—aside from his beautiful laugh.

"You aren't a diversion," he said. "Not at all."

"Okay. Well, that's good." She forced herself to maintain eye contact while asking the one question she wasn't sure she wanted answered. "When are you going back?"

His lips pulled into a smirk. "I'm not."

Her heart started to pound. Was he staying? Did he mean Earth in general, or with her? And why the hell was she already thinking in long-term…terms with him?

With utmost care, he slowly pulled his hips away, then slid his dick back into her. Her eyes started to roll shut as tendrils of pleasure wound through her body.

Okay, yeah, that was part of it. But not all.

The sense of potential that surrounded him—surrounded *them*—was stronger than anything she'd experienced before. She wanted a chance to explore it. To explore *him*. And not just his magnificent body.

"You've shown me that Earth has much to offer." His eyes seemed to glitter as his smirk deepened.

Smug bastard. Maybe she *was* the only one interested in things beyond the physical.

"Yeah. We Earth girls can be a lot of fun."

She turned away, no longer wanting to see the look in his eyes. With her neck bared to him, he ran his tongue along its length, catching her earlobe between his teeth gently, as she'd done to him.

Damn, he was good at that. At all of this.

She shivered in response, her body remaining open to him even as she tried to shutter her heart. For someone new to being human, he sure was catching on fast.

"I've met many 'Earth girls'," he said.

Now she was confused. "What?"

He chuckled again, nipping at her neck and suckling her flesh. "Did you think I'd just crashed here or something?"

"Well... Yeah. Or something."

"I've been on Earth for several years. If I'd wanted to explore sex or coffee or video games, I could easily have done so."

"Why didn't you?"

He bit her neck harder, raking his teeth along her skin in a way that set goosebumps flying along her arms and legs. Her core clenched around him involuntarily.

"It never occurred to me to try," he said. "Until you."

Her heart pounded harder. That was the nicest, sexiest thing anyone had ever said to her.

Rather than let herself get swept up in the sentiment, she tried to keep herself grounded. Which wasn't easy, with him teasing the skin of her neck and the feel of his thick length buried within her.

"What did you do with your time?" she said.

"I was hunting down rogue aliens who aren't supposed to be here."

"Oh my God. There are more of you?"

"No."

He pushed himself up so he could hold her gaze as she turned to face him. The intense, predatory cast was back in his eyes.

"There is only one of me," he said. "And be very glad for that."

A shiver ran through her. She didn't want to look too closely at the implications of that statement—of what kind of alien he was, or had been.

"But there are other aliens on Earth?" she said.

"Yes."

"And you're some kind of...space cop, hunting them down?"

He snorted. "There are some who would see it that way."

"But not you."

His smirk deepened. He did another of those long strokes with his dick, shifting his hips back, then slamming into her. Again and again.

Damn, what had they been talking about? The pleasure was rocking against her brain, just like his body rocked against hers. Eroding her defenses.

He quickened his pace, grinding his pelvis against her clit every time he landed. There was purpose in his gaze. He pushed himself up on his hands, angling himself to land deeper. He was taking them to the edge and ready to leap right off of it with her.

Two could play at this game. She clenched her core around his dick, gripping him as hard as she could. Just for kicks, she added a little shimmy-twist to her hips as she rocked against him.

The extra friction turned the tendrils of pleasure coursing through her body into torrents. He let out a groan, slamming into her faster. He didn't hold anything back. She couldn't believe she could take it—could meet his passion and match it.

The lightning finally struck, arcing along her nerve endings and setting everything on fire. Her skin, her muscles, her bones. Her heartbeat was thunder, increasing the pleasure, the ecstasy of the moment. And he was right there with her.

Glowing silver light flashed along his scars, growing brighter as he kept thrusting into her. It was almost too much to look at. The lights pulsed faster until a flash nearly blinded her as he yelled her name.

Her name. Not some weird alien expletive.

The aftershocks of her orgasm relit into a pounding beat that matched the throbbing of his dick within her. He kept pumping, as if he was trying to experience every ounce of pleasure their bodies could possibly give. His arms were trembling when he finally stopped, his dick pushed firmly into her.

"Brooke," he moaned.

Sweat beaded across his forehead. He lowered his lips to hers, another moan sounding low in his throat as he tasted her, sank into her again, his tongue languidly stroking hers. He finally released her mouth, his hips shifting against hers in a move that made her body echo the pleasure he'd just given her. It was like the afterimage of the lines of silver along his body that was still fading from her retinas.

He rolled off of her, but didn't let her go. She tucked herself into his side, trailing her fingertip through his chest hair. While she did, he grabbed the blanket from the couch and pulled it down over her.

"You were chilled earlier," he said.

Damn. He was a keeper. And she *could* keep him. He was going to stay.

It seemed a little weird that a cop would be so willing to give up protecting people, though. Most of the ones she'd met were more dedicated to the job. Maybe he was trying to get away from a bad situation. If he'd been ripped apart, she could see him wanting a different line of work.

She let out a laugh, and said, "My mom will be so happy that I'm dating a cop. Just leave out the 'space' part."

"I didn't say I was part of law enforcement. I said there were some who would see it that way."

The happy bubble her thoughts had been building around her brain popped. A feeling of misgiving took its place.

"Then what are you?" she said.

"Were."

"What?"

"I'm not what I was when I came to this planet."

"Fine," she said. "What *were* you?"

He was quiet for a moment. Then he said, "A bounty hunter. And assassin."

"Assassin?"

"That's the closest word for it in your language."

A contract killer. She was fucking an alien contract killer. And she *had feelings* for him.

Her seeming superpower of finding the most messed up guy possible and then falling for him had landed her in bad situations before. Elliot the ever-annoying was a prime example. But this?

This took it to a whole new level.

Chapter Ten

"Something is wrong."

Zemanni had been holding Brooke in his arms, feeling more at peace with the universe than he ever had. That contentment had been shattered when she practically leapt away from him, hurrying to the kitchen. He'd followed her, and was standing in the open archway, watching as she gathered her clothes and dressed.

"Nothing's wrong." The strain in her voice made plain that she was lying.

"I told you that I *used* to be those things. I'm not anymore."

"Right. Because you're trapped in human form."

Did she think that if he could go back to his natural form that he'd pursue the same objectives?

Wouldn't he?

He wasn't sure anymore. That thought alone was extremely unsettling.

"I'm not just trapped in human form," he said. "I'm *this* human. Eric Peterson."

"Who the hell is he?"

Zemanni wasn't sure how to describe the human whose DNA had already started overwriting his personality before he became stuck in this form. He settled on, "A very strong-willed man."

"Okay." She pulled her shirt into place, then glared at him. "Wait a minute. You didn't kill him to take his place, did you?"

"No." He left out the part where he'd *tried* to kill Eric— and failed. It didn't seem like it would go over well. And it was embarrassing.

"I've heard others say that protecting people is hardwired into Eric's DNA," Zemanni said. "I didn't think such a thing was possible, but his form had started affecting me even before I became trapped in it."

"Again, not doing so great on the reassuring."

"What do you want me to say? That I've changed? That I'm no longer a killer? Because the first is true, but the second…" He let his voice trail off. His chest felt tight and his skin prickled unpleasantly. "I've never lied to you, Brooke. I don't intend to start now."

"Wow. So you admit that you would kill people."

"To protect you, I would. And even from the limited experience I have with you, I'm pretty sure you would kill to protect others, too."

"That's not the same thing."

"I can't go back and change the past. This is my present. And I'm trying to focus on my future."

"I have to go."

"Where?"

The prickling along his skin blossomed into warning klaxons. If she was planning on going to the authorities, it might be best for him to leave. But he didn't *want* to leave.

He wanted to spend more time with her, to get to know her. Everything they'd experienced together so far had utterly fascinated him. Even in such a short time, he felt connected to her. And he was actually glad for that.

"I have some neighbors who are homebound." At his quizzical expression, she said, "They can't leave their apartment. They have nurses who check on them, but they like my cooking and I bring them meals most evenings."

She stalked to the fridge and threw open the door, grabbing a large dish covered in foil. "It's just another aspect of my stupid rescuer nature manifesting itself."

"What?"

"Forget it. My mom is a shrink. She likes to psychoanalyze why I'm such a total failure."

Rage tore through him at Brooke's words. He felt his lips pull back from his teeth in a snarl. Brooke looked surprised, but she didn't flinch away from him.

"She should not say such things of you," he said.

The corner of Brooke's mouth twitched up for a fraction of a second, but then she scowled. "I'd tell you to take it up with her, but I don't want you to fucking *kill* her."

So that was the sticking point. She didn't like that he'd

killed people. It wasn't too surprising, knowing what he did of Earth's culture.

"I only killed my assigned targets."

Unless he happened across a lucrative bounty in the process. Like the Lyrians—as much good as pursuing them had done for him.

Then again, if it weren't for his encounter with the pair and their bizarre ad hoc family, he wouldn't have met Brooke and enjoyed the physical pursuits that she'd shared with him that day. Having to reassemble himself had only sped the changes that Eric's DNA had begun.

Sentients used to pass through Zemanni's awareness like static against the background of his environment. The only ones that he ever felt he could truly focus on were threats, targets, and opportunities. No one else felt…real.

But after trying to obtain the Cygnian hybrid known as Sorca and taking Eric Peterson's DNA into his body to do so, his *personality* had started to change. Zemanni found himself taking on Eric's form when others would do just as well, because he actually liked noticing other people.

It had been unnerving at first. He'd tried to play it off as research so that he could assimilate more thoroughly. Deep down, he knew better.

"Were they bad people?" Brooke's voice was thin and weak, but still enough to bring all of his focus back to her. He'd never heard her sound so…timid.

"I don't know."

He'd known Brooke wouldn't like his answer. He hadn't known how his heart would seem to lose its rhythm when he noticed tears form in her eyes.

"I didn't care before." Dammit, why couldn't he lie to her?

She glared at him, which was oddly encouraging.

"'Before'," she said. "What about now?"

"Now… I don't know."

"Great. Let me know when you figure that out."

She hit him with her shoulder as she stalked from the room. He could have stopped her. He was still considering it.

Part of him felt profoundly unsettled at the thought of her leaving when she was so angry. His lungs strained to draw in air and his abdomen felt like it was housing a nest of skeelbats.

He wasn't overly concerned about her sending authorities after him, knowing what he did of Eric's status on Earth. But Zemanni couldn't keep himself from wondering if Brooke would come back. His stomach cramped painfully at the thought of her walking out the door and never returning.

She paused at the door. "Put the chain in place behind me. My stupid ex has a key and likes to let himself in when I'm not home. And don't open the door for anyone but me."

She would be back. And she was taking precautions to keep Zemanni safe. With what she had learned, it surprised him that she still cared.

She *cared.*

Instead of thinking about how he could use that to his advantage, his focus was on how the fluttery feeling in his gut grew in inverse proportion to the tightness in his chest decreasing. He could breathe again and he felt lighter somehow. How did anyone function with such attention-demanding forms?

Brooke didn't look back as she slammed the door shut behind her. He could hear her quick steps on the stairs that led from her apartment.

He locked the door and secured it with the chain, as she'd instructed. Then he smiled.

He could make this work. He would *enjoy* making this work. They would be mated. And he would see to it that she enjoyed their bonding every bit as much as he did.

He headed for the bathroom and gathered the clothes that he had stolen after escaping the forest confrontation with the Lyrians. He would need more. As he dressed, he considered his options for obtaining Earth resources.

Managing his identity could be a problem. Zemanni considered it highly probable that Eric had joined Sorca in returning to Sadr-4 to attempt to convince the High Council of the Coalition to recognize Earth's First Contact committee.

Zemanni doubted they would succeed, which meant that Eric would very likely receive a mind-wipe and completely forget his new bondmate when he was sent back to Earth. Or he might remain on Sadr-4, working to further his homeworld's best interests.

Assuming Eric's identity on Earth would be problematic. Without being able to assume different identities, it would be a near impossible challenge for Zemanni to gather enough information to fool Eric's colleagues in this country's government. And the attempt would separate Zemanni from Brooke.

No, he'd find another way to contribute to supporting them both. He could always approach Earth's First Contact committee…

The front door rattled as someone inserted a key in the lock. His heart picked up. Brooke was back already.

Except she had told him to put the chain in place. Why would she be trying to unlock the door when she thought Zemanni had secured it from the other side?

He walked out of the bathroom, watching as the door opened as far as the chain would let it.

"What the hell?" The male voice grated on Zemanni's ears. Even worse was the sound of the chain rubbing against the door as the man tried to force it open.

"Brooke?" he said. "Open the door. How did you even get back in here without me seeing you?"

Zemanni felt like his body had flooded with fire. This human had been watching Brooke. Stalking her, like prey.

Zemanni recognized the signs of a hunter—of a *threat*.

He approached the door, waiting for the man to have his fingers wrapped around the wood as he tried for a better grip.

Idiot.

Zemanni kicked the door shut with enough force to severely bruise the man's fingers. Not break—or sever—them. Brooke would be okay with this level of damage to her 'ex'. Hopefully.

The screaming was the most grating sound of all. It might also attract unwanted attention.

Zemanni slid the chain free, then opened the door and reached out to the human. Grabbing *his* prey by the front of his coat, Zemanni pulled him into the apartment and shut the door behind them.

"Stop making that sound," Zemanni said.

The human stared up at him with wide eyes. His dark hair was thick with grease and hung past his shoulders. His bangs were long enough to obscure his vision.

"Idiot" seemed too kind a term.

At least the man stopped screaming. He cradled his hand to his chest.

"You will leave Brooke alone." Zemanni kept his grip on the man's coat, lifting him partway off the ground.

"Who the fuck are you?"

"I'm her mate."

"Mate?" The guy managed to laugh, but it was somehow an angry sound. "That cheating bitch. But she's *my* cheating bitch."

Zemanni knew what that word meant in this context. He didn't know it would make his vision go white with rage.

Oblivious to his danger, the man went on. "She's meant to be with me. And I'm going to make her realize it."

Zemanni shook the man, hard. "If you wish to keep your hands, you will never raise them in harm toward her. If you wish to keep your skin, you will never even *think* of touching her. And if you wish to keep your tongue, you will never use it to speak ill of her again."

The human paled, but still sneered at Zemanni. "You can't threaten me like that."

"It isn't a threat. I'm informing you of the consequences of your choices." Zemanni leaned in closer, and said, "Choose well."

Chapter Eleven

When Brooke returned to the apartment, Zemanni was playing the same video game she'd shown him earlier. It was a little too reminiscent of Elliot. She could almost imagine his body-funk smell lingering near the stairs.

But the guy sitting on her couch wasn't one of the string of losers she'd dated. He was a dangerous alien assassin. And she had a freaking crush on him.

"My neighbor sent home a pair of shoes for you." She dropped everything she was carrying on the table near the door and locked the deadbolt behind her, then latched the chain into place.

Part of her had wondered if Z would still be here when she returned. She had to admit that she was relieved he hadn't left.

"I see you put on some clothes," she said, joining him on the couch.

He grunted in response. Damn, was he turning into another boyfriend that would ignore her in favor of video games? Elliot had been terrible about that.

"You don't have to worry about your ex anymore," Z

said. He kept his attention on the screen, zapping alien mechas.

Her stomach lurched. "What did you do?"

"Nothing permanent. He won't be playing video games for a while, though."

She grabbed Z's controller, then tossed it on the coffee table. "What did you do, Z?"

Instead of being mad at her interruption, Zemanni smiled at her.

"Do you have any idea how much I enjoy it when you call me that?" he said.

This time, the fluttering in her stomach was pleasant. It clashed with her worry, though, leaving her feeling confused and vaguely guilty.

"Stop being charming and answer my question."

"Charming, huh?" He leaned forward and turned off the TV, then pushed the table away from the couch with his foot.

"Oh, no. We are not doing that again until I know what happened with you and Elliot."

"He came by looking for trouble."

"Please don't say he found it."

Z shrugged, then his expression darkened. She knew she should be scared—any sane person would be scared. Instead, she felt a shiver down her spine and her arms broke out in gooseflesh.

"Mom is right," she said. "I am so messed up."

"Brooke, I know a predator when I see one. From intimate experience."

Right. Because he was one. Or used to be—she hoped.

"Elliot was harmless."

"He was not." The force in Z's voice killed the argument she'd been about to make. "The things he said and what he was doing—keeping your keys, watching your place—"

"He was watching my place?"

That was creepy. And she'd had no idea.

"He won't be back," Z said.

"I guess I should thank you."

Z grinned, leaning toward her. She put a hand on his chest to stop him. Well, to hold him off for a few minutes. There were a few things she still wanted to understand.

Someone pounded on the door and she jumped. Z was on his feet in an instant.

"Police," a muffled voice called from the other side of the door. "We need to talk to you."

"Shit," Brooke said. "What did you do?"

"I already told you. Nothing."

"You said 'nothing permanent'. What is 'nothing permanent'?" She jumped again at more pounding on the door. "Go to the bedroom and stay there. I'll handle this."

She ran to the door as Z started toward the hallway. She gave him enough time to be out of sight before looking through the peephole. There were two cops on the other side. She left the chain in place as she opened the door.

"Hi, officer," she said. "How can I help you?"

"We had a report of an assault in this apartment just a little bit ago. Are you alone, ma'am?"

"Actually—"

Before she could finish her sentence, Z appeared behind her. Her cheeks prickled with anger. He was supposed to stay out of sight.

"Actually, I'm staying with her," Z said.

"And you are?" The officer raised an eyebrow, his back stiffening. The one behind him dropped his arms to his sides—nearer to his weapon.

"He's a friend." Brooke tried to step between Z and the officers, but he pushed her out of the way.

"Do you have a fingerprint scanner?" Z said.

The officer seemed a little confused. He glanced over his shoulder at his partner, who nodded.

"Yeah." The closer officer took out his phone and held it up.

Z held up both hands to show they were empty, then slowly reached forward and pressed his thumb to the screen. What the hell was he playing at?

The officer looked at his screen, his eyes practically bugging out of his head at whatever he was reading. He turned and showed the screen to the other officer, whose mouth dropped open.

"We're so sorry, Agent Peterson," the first officer said. "We get reports, we have to run them down."

"Of course." Zemanni's voice was weirdly…affable. "But could we maybe keep our voices down. I'd rather not have anyone know I'm here. It seems like the only way I can get an actual vacation is if I keep a very low profile."

"What's a vacation?" The second officer laughed at his own joke.

The first joined him and, to Brooke's shock, so did Z. His eyes crinkled at the corners as he smiled at the pair as if they were all drinking buddies. He was like a totally different person—which unnerved her.

"Again, our apologies," the first officer said.

"Nothing to apologize for, officers." Z gave them a half-wave, half-salute. "We're all on the same side here."

"Yes, sir." The officers turned and headed down the stairs, still beaming.

Z closed the door and locked it, then turned to Brooke. He studied her face for a moment, then said, "What?"

"Okay, the list of things I need you to explain is now about a mile longer."

"Eric Peterson is a special agent with your country's government."

Brooke stared at him. Her brain seemed to be stuck in neutral.

"I think I need to sit down," she said.

Z gestured to the couch. He followed after her and sat at her side. She stared at him for a long time before speaking.

"So, *did* you assault Elliot?"

"I kicked the door shut. If he hadn't been trying to break in, his fingers wouldn't have been injured."

"Ouch. Are you sure he's okay?"

"He was fine when he left."

Brooke stared at him. She was getting sick of his half-truths and evasions.

Z let out a sigh. "I'm sure I didn't harm him grievously. I can't say what state he's in now. The guy is an idiot."

She couldn't argue that point.

"This is all so weird."

"*You* think it's weird? At least you're in your natural form. This body has so many bladders, I can hardly keep track of them all."

She laughed. She couldn't believe it, but she did. Sitting on the couch with an alien assassin.

"You told me that you didn't used to care who you killed. And you said you *were* an assassin. Past tense. What about now?"

"Now… It's a lot more complicated. But in some ways, more simple."

"How?"

He leaned forward and kissed her.

Chapter Twelve

Zemanni could get used to being human. Pursuing contingency plans for escaping this form no longer seemed important. He rolled over on Brooke's bed, reaching out for her. The sheets were warm, but empty.

He sat up and glanced around. Morning light streamed into the room. They must have finally fallen asleep at some point in the night. She hadn't mentioned needing to go to work the next day, but maybe she had gone and didn't want to wake him.

He heard soft voices in the other room. Maybe not.

He swung his legs over the bed, grabbing his jeans and sliding them on. As he fastened them, he headed for the open bedroom door. Peering around its edge, he saw Brooke talking to Elliot just inside the apartment.

Zemanni grabbed his shirt and swung it on, buttoning it as quickly—and quietly—as he could. He went back to his position, listening.

"I just wanted to apologize in person," Elliot said. "I was an ass. You deserved a lot better than that."

What the hell? Was he trying to get back in her good

graces?

"Thank you, Elliot. It means a lot to me to hear you say that."

Crap, was it working?

The now-familiar feeling of possessiveness stirred in his chest again. Zemanni strode out of the bedroom. Brooke turned to him and smiled. He barely registered it, too busy glaring at Elliot—who smirked at him.

Zemanni was going to knock that smirk off Elliot's face and give him a bruise to match the ones on his fingers. Except...

Zemanni slowed his approach. Something was different about Elliot today. Something was wrong. His hair was washed, for one. He was wearing the same outfit as yesterday, but it was clean, too.

"Z, Elliot just came here to apologize," Brooke said. "You can stop looking at him like you're going to pick him up and use him to club something."

"Yeah. Okay."

She seemed taken aback at how easily Zemanni had calmed down. He was too busy processing whatever this new feeling was that his human body was feeding him.

His pulse was pounding, senses hyper-alert. He experienced something similar in his natural form—a preparation for battle—when facing a threat. But Elliot wasn't dangerous at all.

Elliot brushed his long bangs behind one ear—with the

same fingers that Zemanni had smashed in the doorway the day before. Fingers that had miraculously healed.

"Brooke," Zemanni said. "Step away from him."

"I told you, he's just here to apologize."

"Brooke, please."

"Please?" Elliot let out a disgusted snort. "I never thought I would witness the great Blorvo Zemanni begging another sentient for anything."

"Blorvo?" Brooke said.

"It's an ancestral name." Zemanni inched closer, hoping to keep this newcomer distracted for long enough to get close and— And what? Protect Brooke?

Trapped in this form, there was nothing he could do. Not against another Scorpiian.

"Wait a minute. How does *he* know your full name and I don't?"

Don't think about it. Don't figure it out.

Her eyes widened and she turned toward "Elliot" and smiled.

"You're another Scorpiian," she said. "Like Zemanni."

Vapor pits.

She wasn't done digging her hole. "Why do you look like Elliot, though? I mean, that form will get you nowhere."

The Scorpiian looked to Zemanni. "She knows about us? You *told* her about us?"

"I can explain," Zemanni said.

"Please do. Right after I dispatch this Earthling."

Brooke finally realized the danger she was in. She quickly backed away from the Scorpiian, but it pulled out a stasis disc and activated it, freezing her in place.

"Are you done with her?" it said.

Zemanni had to think quickly. He couldn't let the newcomer know how far gone he was, or he would lose any kind of influence over the situation.

How had another Scorpiian arrived so quickly to take over Zemanni's contracts on Earth? His ship had only been destroyed a few days ago. It didn't send a distress signal. He wasn't checking in with anyone. This Scorpiian must have already been in the area. It must have been waiting for Zemanni to…

His stomach clenched painfully as missing pieces fell into place. Zemanni had been distracted after assimilating Eric's DNA. He'd been off his game. And he'd blamed that for the Sadirians being able to find him. For the Lyrians destroying his ship.

But maybe he hadn't been as far off as he thought. Maybe someone had been sabotaging him. It was just the kind of thing another Scorpiian would do to try to make their name—and steal his bounties on Earth.

A young Scorpiian. Ruled by greed. Zemanni could work with this. He only hoped Brooke would forgive him if they made it out alive.

"Now that you're here, I don't need her anymore,"

Zemanni said. "But you can't kill her."

Brooke's eyes filled with tears. He could see the tendons along her neck pulling in strain as she tried to free herself from the stasis field. Ever a fighter.

"Do you want to do it yourself?" it said. "There's no bounty on her, so it doesn't matter."

"Killing her is inefficient." Zemanni forced his voice to be cold and even. "If she goes missing, the authorities will look for her. I assume they'll already soon be looking for Elliot?"

The Scorpiian shrugged. "From what I gathered in my limited time with him, I doubt anyone will be upset enough by his absence to even report it."

Brooke would be. Even knowing that Elliot had been a danger to her.

Zemanni had someone's death in mind—but not another Earthling's.

"Identify yourself," Zemanni said.

"Kagnan."

"Your presence on Earth violates my rights as sole operator on this planet. Explain."

Kagnan shrugged. "I picked up a faint energy reading from your ship, as if its cloaking generator was slightly out of phase. It inspired my curiosity."

Zemanni just bet it did. He also would bet that Kagnan was behind the misalignment in his system in the first place. There was an external vent that could grant access to the peripheral systems of the cloak given the right circumstances.

"I discovered a few remains of your ship," Kagnan said. "Don't worry, I took care of them for you."

"I take it they're now sitting in your own vessel's hold?"

Kagnan smiled. "I did need something to provide proof that Earth is open for assignment."

"Not quite yet," Zemanni said.

"You can't fault me for believing you were dead. I also found a significant amount of quicksilver in the area."

"It takes more than that to kill me."

"Most impressive."

Trying to use false flattery on *him*? Kagnan was such an amateur.

Zemanni kept his tone cold. "I had secured a base of operations with this Earthling and was working toward making contact with one of the groups of sentients on the planet who have a means of communicating with Scorpii-2."

It was what most Scorpiians would do in a similar situation. Zemanni had already dismissed the idea. He *preferred* to stay on Earth. He was enjoying this form too much—and Brooke's company. If only there was a way he could communicate his plan to her, to let her know that he wasn't actually planning to betray her. He was trying to keep her safe.

"It's a good thing I'm here, then," Kagnan said. "I can

send a signal for you."

For a price, Zemanni was sure. He couldn't let Kagnan get the upper hand in their negotiations.

"I will send my own signal," Zemanni said. "Using your equipment—for a fee. And I will also need to use your programming pod."

"Do you need to upgrade your knowledge of Earth's customs?"

"Of course not," Zemanni said. "The Earthling needs a mind-wipe."

Kagnan nodded. "The use of that equipment will be expensive."

"It will be free." Before Kagnan could complain, Zemanni said, "And I will not report that you are on Earth when I am still the designated operator."

He wanted to muddy Kagnan's feelings—to throw Kagnan off *its* game. The fine for encroaching on another's hunting grounds could ruin a Scorpiian who was just starting out. And while Kagnan's thoughts were on its resources, Zemanni could begin to bait his trap.

"There is another matter," Zemanni said.

Kagnan glared at him. "Which is?"

"You have a backup store of quicksilver, correct?"

"Of course."

"I wish to purchase it."

As expected, Kagnan's face lit up. Quicksilver was the most precious resource among their kind. Zemanni could replace his ship for the same cost as replacing his quicksilver. And Kagnan knew it.

"These circumstances are highly unusual," Kagnan said.

Again, his behavior aligned completely with Zemanni's expectations. If this persisted, Zemanni would have no difficulty keeping Brooke safe.

"I understand that," Zemanni said. "Which is why I will pay you half again as much as its worth."

Kagnan's smile deepened. It thought it had Zemanni at a disadvantage. But then, no one knew how many resources Zemanni had been able to secure over his long lifespan. And no other Scorpiian could conceive of him being so willing to part with them.

"We can negotiate on our way to your ship," Zemanni said. "Right now, we need to address the issue of the Earthling."

"I thought you didn't want to kill her."

"I don't."

"Then what could we possibly do about her now?"

"We'll need transportation to your ship. Rendering her unconscious and carrying her to her car will appear suspicious to anyone who might see us. She needs to come with us of her own will."

Kagnan snorted. "Good luck with that. From what I've seen so far, these sentients are highly unreasonable."

Zemanni would have gone with "passionate". He didn't argue the case. Instead, he turned to Brooke, hiding any sign of sympathy or regret from his features—even though they weighed heavily on his heart.

If he shifted his body so that Kagnan couldn't see his face, Zemanni wouldn't be able to keep track of Kagnan's movements. And Kagnan was still very much a threat to them. When this was all over—when they were safe— Zemanni would explain. He only hoped Brooke would understand.

"Brooke."

Her eyes were the only thing she could move in the stasis field. The skin around them crinkled as she tried to glare at him, no doubt. The tears he had seen before were gone.

"You've heard all that has passed between us," Zemanni said. "Do as I say, and you will have a chance to return to your life as it was. You won't remember me or any of this. But understand that Kagnan will not hesitate to kill you with very little provocation. Do not scream. Do not run."

Zemanni nodded to Kagnan, who turned off the stasis field. Immediately, Brooke lashed out, her fist flying toward Zemanni.

He considered letting it connect. It would no doubt help her feel better. But it would weaken him in Kagnan's perception, and Zemanni couldn't have that. He caught her wrist, twisting it around and pulling her up against his chest.

She writhed against him, and he had to clamp down on

his body's reaction to her. Her scent, her heat. If Kagnan had any idea of how much Zemanni cared for her, they would both be in much greater danger.

"Brooke," he said. "Stop struggling."

After a few more thrashes, she went still. She looked up at him, her eyes filled with fire, and spat in his face.

"You bastard." Her voice was low and raw.

"I've never said otherwise." Zemanni kept his hold on her, waiting to see how Kagnan would react.

"These things are disgusting," it said. "I can't wait to wipe her and be rid of her."

"The sooner you both are out of my life and brain, the better." She shoved away from Zemanni, and he let her go.

He kept his face impassive as his heart seemed to crumple in on itself within his chest.

Chapter Thirteen

"Quicksilver first."

If Brooke heard Zemanni harp about the fucking quicksilver much more, she'd throw *herself* in the "programming pod" that Kagnan was so eager to get her into. She'd been listening to the two of them argue for the last half-hour as she drove them out of town to the sparsely forested field where Kagnan had hidden his ship.

She should be excited. Curious. Frightened, for God's sake. She was sitting in an alien vessel, arms and legs crossed as she glared at the two men in front of her.

Kagnan wanted to erase Brooke's brain first, then send a signal to the other Scorpiians, then give Zemanni some quicksilver. Zemanni wanted to do it in reverse order. And, of course, Kagnan wanted to be paid before anything else happened.

"Not until you have transferred the resources we agreed upon," Kagnan said. Again. "We should get rid of the Earthling first."

"Oh my God," Brooke said. "Just transfer half of what you agreed on, then get your quicksilver, then transfer the rest and send your stupid signal."

Both men turned and stared at her.

"What?" she said.

Z's lips quirked up a bit. "That's actually a good idea."

"Strange." Kagnan cocked his head to the side as he looked at Brooke. "Surprising that it came from her."

Brooke covered her face with her hands. "I can't wait to forget this conversation."

Except, she could. As much as she'd said the opposite earlier, she wasn't eager to forget Zemanni. What the hell was wrong with her?

There was even a tiny part of her brain that kept telling her that this was all a trick he was playing on Kagnan. That Z was trying to get them both out of this alive and with their memories intact.

He'd saved her life already, right? He could have just let Kagnan kill her. Like Kagnan had killed Elliot.

She was glad her face was covered. Of everything she'd experienced since Z came into her life, that was the part she had the most trouble believing was real.

Sure, Elliot was an asshole with delusions of stalkerhood. But Brooke could have handled him. Maybe even—

She stopped her utterly useless train of thought. Elliot was past her ability to help him now.

Always a rescuer.

"Without quicksilver, I can't make the transfer," Z said.

"You can if you give me your code."

Brooke dropped her hands to her lap. "Ugh, this is the most boring alien abduction ever. How about a simultaneous exchange? You know, like you both meet partway across a bridge?"

When they both stared at her again, she let out another grunt of frustration. "Get out the quicksilver and let him have it the moment he gives you the code you need. Haven't you done anything like this before?"

"This sort of situation doesn't really come up," Z said.

She glared at him for having the nerve to address her directly. She was also weirdly relieved that he was still talking to her, especially since Kagnan only talked *about* her.

Wasn't there something about surviving by making the kidnappers see you as a person? Except they weren't the same kind of people, and she wasn't entirely sure she *wanted* them to see her as a fellow Scorpiian.

Kagnan turned to the wall of his ship and pressed his hand on its surface. His skin rippled, then glowed with a bright silver light. His flesh seemed to melt, flowing into the control.

No wonder Z was so eager to get his quicksilver back. It looked like the Scorpiians' technology revolved around their shapeshifting abilities.

A panel opened in the wall, revealing a clear cylindrical container filled with liquid that looked like mercury.

"Huh," Brooke said.

Z glanced over at her. "What?"

She shrugged. "It's just like in the movies."

Kagnan ignored her. He set the container on the floor, then held out his hand to Z.

"The code?" Kagnan said.

Z reached down for the container. As he did, he held his hand above Kagnan's. A single drop of shining silver liquid dropped from Z's hand onto Kagnan's.

"Gross," Brooke said. "Was that like your DNA or something?" She remembered reading about genetic codes back in high school.

Z glared at her as he backed away from Kagnan. She wasn't sure who she should focus on.

Z opened the cylinder and shoved his hand inside. The silver fluid crawled up his arm, wrapping around it as it flowed into his skin. He shivered, and not in a good way. She knew when something felt good to him, and this didn't. Somehow, the thought was encouraging.

When the container was empty, he let it fall to the floor of the ship. The lines of silver that she had traced repeatedly the night before started to glow so bright, she could see them clearly through his clothing.

Meanwhile, Kagnan was still standing with his arm embedded in his ship. His eyes widened suddenly.

"There's so much here," he said.

"Yeah, I've been busy." Z walked to the other side of the

room and placed a hand over one of the weird access ports. His fingers, wrist, and part of his arm glowed silver, becoming near liquid as they flowed into the ship's control.

The tiny bit of hope she'd been feeling vanished. She had sort of wanted it to not work. She'd wanted Z to stay… Z. Now he was an alien, and—

Kagnan suddenly stood straighter. His body twitched as if a current was running through it. His skin blackened, like paper being consumed by a flame. He made a tiny grunting noise, and then fell to the ground, his arm still stuck in the wall. Wisps of smoke came out of the top of his head.

"What the hell?" Brooke was on her feet, hands up, ready to defend herself. Against what, she wasn't sure.

"Calm down," Z said.

"I will not calm down. Did you just kill that guy?"

He glared at her. "Yes."

"What? How?"

"I distracted him by offering him what he wanted. He was so focused on my resources, that he didn't notice the failsafe he had activated by using an incomplete genetic sample."

"But you said you gave him the code he needed."

"It was incomplete. Most Scorpiians aren't capable of giving a partial genetic sample, and so it's used as our primary means of identification. He wouldn't have guessed that what I gave him would activate security countermeasures."

Brooke looked at the charred body hanging from the wall.

"Scorpiians take their resources very seriously." Z retracted his arm from the wall. It coalesced into a human-looking hand. "Kagnan also didn't realize how quickly I could reassimilate quicksilver. This amateur had no idea who it was dealing with. Its ship is now mine."

Z approached her—cautiously, as if he thought she might run. If she thought she could escape the ship, she might. Except... She wasn't done here. Not with this. Not with him.

"You lied to him," she said. "You told me you never lie."

He was right in front of her, wall of solid-seeming chest. It was an illusion, she knew.

"I told you that I had never lied to *you.*"

"Well, gosh. Doesn't that just make me special."

She was starting to build up hope, and that was making her feel stupid. This guy was a killer. There was a body of a person he'd just killed in the room with them.

And he was an alien. Absolutely alien, now that he'd gotten some quicksilver back into his system. He was a shapeshifter, and she had no idea what that really meant or what the limits to his abilities might be.

"You are special, Brooke. To me." He lifted her face to his, one hand under her chin.

As he leaned down to her, she said, "I'm not kissing you in the same room as a dead body."

"Right." He stood straight again. "I suppose that's fair."

"I'm so confused right now. I don't know what's going on or what will happen next."

"What's going on is that there was a threat to you. I have neutralized it."

"That's one way of putting it."

"As to what's next, that depends on you." He stepped to the side, blocking her view of Kagnan's blackened form. "Aside from this ruse that saved both of our lives, I truly haven't lied to you. I told you back at your apartment that you would have a choice. You can go back to your life, either with or without your memories of me intact."

"What if I don't like those choices?"

He smiled, then brushed a lock of hair behind her ear. "Haven't you learned yet? I always leave something out."

"Another choice?"

He nodded. "It won't be easy and I'll need your help to pull it off."

"Again. I totally saved your bacon with Kag-man there."

He laughed, and her heart seemed to skip at the sound.

"It would mean that we could stay together," he said.

She shrugged one shoulder, shifting a little closer to his chest.

"I'm listening."

Chapter Fourteen

With the main bay doors open, the hangar was chilly, even with the small ship's heating system trying to fight back the cold air. Brooke sat on a crate that Zemanni had carefully inspected for hazards before letting her use.

"You can still change your mind," he said.

"Shut up."

He smiled, walking toward the open doors with his hands held up. His feet crunched on the snow

"I surrender," he shouted.

The air rippled as a ship decloaked in front of him. It was shaped like a thin crescent moon, with a hull of gleaming black. A standard Sadirian skimmer.

A voice shouted out from a loudspeaker set in its hull. "Do not move."

"I wasn't planning on it."

He heard movement behind him—footsteps on the ramp. Brooke joined him, but she couldn't lift her hands.

She was holding the container of quicksilver.

"I told you to stay inside." Zemanni stepped forward, putting himself between her and the skimmer.

"Yeah, and since when do I do as you say?"

"We said don't move," the voice from the skimmer boomed.

Zemanni let out a sigh. "She's an Earthling. And I am not a threat to you. We need to talk."

The skimmer landed in front of them. Its hatch opened and a ramp descended. Within seconds, two male figures approached. They both wore the silver uniforms of Sadirian soldiers.

One filled his out impressively, his chest bigger than some of the young trees around them. The other was thin and wiry, and walked with a hesitance that no Sadirian soldier would show.

Curious.

The large one held his arm up toward them, pointing his bracer—along with all its weapons—at them. The other didn't.

"Brendan," the big one said. "Your wristband."

"Oh, right." The thinner one held up the wrong arm, then quickly shifted. "Don't try anything," he said.

"Where are you guys getting your soldiers nowadays?" Zemanni said.

"I ask the questions." The big one took a few more cautious steps forward. "You both read as humans, but it wouldn't be hard for Scorpiians to fool our sensors."

"I'm aware," Zemanni said. "But your sensors are correct in this case."

He stepped aside, revealing Brooke—and the canister of quicksilver. When he nodded to her, she set it down on the ground, then they both backed away.

"What is that?" the thin one asked.

The large one tapped on his bracer a few times. He paused, then tapped again, more urgently.

"Quicksilver," he said. "And a lot of it."

He tapped the side of his helmet. The opaque metal broke into inch-wide segments that folded in on themselves before collapsing into the housing around his uniform's neck.

His skin was dark gold, his scalp and face either hairless or shaved. He glared from Zemanni to Brooke and back again.

"Awesome." The thin one hit the control to remove his helmet as well. As soon as it was in its housing, he took a few deep breaths. His bright orange hair made a striking contrast to the snowy background around him. "Those things make me claustrophobic."

"An Earthling?" Zemanni shook his head. It was the only explanation that made sense.

He knew that the Sadirians were working with humans on their First Contact committee. He didn't know they were letting them run around in Sadirian uniforms.

"I'm Brendan." The thin man waved. "And that's Ari."

Ari glanced over his shoulder, casting a glare at Brendan.

"What?" Brendan said.

"I'm Brooke." She stepped forward and waved back. "And this is Blorvo."

"*Zemanni.*"

"It's a family name." She smirked at Zemanni, even when he glared back. "He doesn't like it."

"So, she's definitely human," Brendan said. "Only Earthlings can make aliens glare quite like that."

Brooke laughed.

"Which makes him what?" Ari kept his wristband trained on both of them. "Standing in front of a Scorpiian vessel, holding a container of quicksilver, wearing a friend's face."

"I was kind of wondering about that, myself," Brendan said.

"Change it," Ari said.

"I can't." Zemanni gestured toward the quicksilver. "All of my quicksilver is in there. Well, almost all of it. I had to keep a little bit to hold myself together."

He slowly pulled down the collar of his shirt, letting Ari see the scars around his neck. "I hear you've let the Lyrians join your group. How's that working out for you?"

"Actually—" Brendan said.

Ari interrupted him. "I said *I* ask the questions. I'm just…kind of stumped about where to start."

"Let me help you," Zemanni said.

"Scorpiians don't help anyone." Ari said. "Not for free."

"True. But I'm not a typical example of my kind." Zemanni gestured toward the huge Sadirian, and said, "I'm guessing you know something about what that's like?"

Ari's glare intensified. Zemanni knew it was a gamble to try to connect with Ari on such a sensitive subject, but it was the only thing he could think of that they had in common. They were both what their people would consider "glitches".

Zemanni tried a different approach. "You're looking for sentients who aren't supposed to be on Earth. So was I."

"We're trying to help them," Brendan said. "Not skin them."

"Oh my God, did you try to skin somebody?" Brooke said.

"I'll explain later." Right after he came up with a plan for how he was going to get the Lyrians to not tear him apart again as soon as they saw him.

"You can't believe anything he tells you," Ari said. "Scorpiians are masters of deceit."

Brooke crossed her arms. "I know. But Zemanni doesn't lie to me."

"Unless he's lying about not lying," Brendan said.

"I'm not lying to any of you. I know I have choices and actions to atone for, but I *am* interested in helping you."

"Why? What's in it for you?" Ari said.

"Protection for myself and my mate." He gestured toward Brooke.

"Mate?" She dropped her arms and smiled at him. "I'm your mate?"

"Again, now is not the time," Zemanni said.

"What is it about these Earthlings?" Ari muttered, shaking his head.

It seemed a good sign that he hadn't disintegrated either of them. Zemanni tried to push the matter further.

"I have changed. Give me a chance to prove it to you."

"How?" Ari had lowered his arm a bit, but brought his wristband back into firing position as Zemanni slowly reached for the front pocket of his shirt.

"I have removed all of the quicksilver from my system that I don't need to survive," he said. "I'm trapped in this human form unless I receive an infusion."

"Which is sitting right in front of you," Ari said.

"I could have escaped with Brooke and this ship. But I stayed. I intend to give this quicksilver to the Department of Homeworld Security. I will only be able to resume my shapeshifting abilities when and where you deem appropriate. I'm putting myself at your disposal, in exchange for you keeping Brooke and I safe."

"And also providing meals to a really sweet elderly couple that lives in my apartment building," Brooke said.

Zemanni glanced at her.

She met his gaze without flinching. "What? They depend on me. You said Brendan has money and could hire them a private chef or something if we had to leave."

"Sure, I can—" Brendan stopped and cleared his throat when Ari glared at him again. "But first, finish your demonstration."

Zemanni pulled out the small pocketknife he'd borrowed from Brooke. He cautiously opened it, not making any sudden moves with Ari's weapons trained on him. Zemanni rolled up his left sleeve, then cut a shallow line along his forearm.

Thin, red blood flowed from the wound. He held it out for Ari to see.

"Okay, that seems legit," Brendan said.

Brooke nodded. "That *is* how they do it in scifi movies."

"We need more than…" Ari's voice trailed off, his gaze fixed on the red seeping from Zemanni's wound. He ran a hand over his face, lowering his other arm to his side. "Actually, that's pretty convincing. Scorpiians don't bleed."

"Well, unless an angry Lyrian rips them into pieces." Brendan shrugged when Ari glared at him. "What? Henry and I are BFFs and he told me all about it."

Brooke took off her scarf and started wrapping it around Zemanni's forearm. He folded the knife and put it back in his pocket.

"Does that mean you'll help us?" Brooke said. "And let us help you?"

"A Scorpiian working with the Department of Homeworld Security," Ari said.

Brendan inched toward them, his attention on the

cylinder. "It was his mission to hunt down the sentients that were on Earth without permission. And let's face it, we could use all the help we can get finding them and sorting out the good guys from the bad."

Ari shook his head, glaring at Zemanni. "You won't be loyal to us. Don't think you have me fooled on that point."

"You know the man whose form I'm wearing," Zemanni said. "When I try to revert to my natural form, this is now the shape I take. His DNA has altered me as much as Brooke has."

"I don't know how I feel about that," Brooke said.

Zemanni pressed on, sensing that they were close to the beginnings of a...bond with this group. "I'm loyal to Brooke and—"

"And I'm loyal to Earth." She shrugged. "Plus I love helping people. From what Zemanni has told me about you guys, that's what you all do."

Brendan smiled broadly. He patted Ari on the shoulder, then reached down and picked up the container of quicksilver. "I'm going to go call Kira."

Ari sighed. "If our planetary liaison says you can join us, I can't go against her orders. But I *will* be watching you, Scorpiian."

"I have no doubt about that."

"So, that's it?" Brooke said. "Because if we're going to be waiting around for a while, I'm going to do it inside where it's warm."

"I'll join you." Zemanni started after her, but paused and turned back to Ari. "My loyalty isn't just to Brooke. It's also to Earth. It feels like... It feels like my homeworld now."

Ari shook his head. "It has that effect on many sentients, it seems. But I can't help but wonder how long it will last."

Zemanni smiled. "As long as she'll have me. And as long as there's work to be done."

Epilogue

"What is it about this planet?" Ari shook his head, gazing out at the mountainside through the windows of the mansion where the Department of Homeworld Security was headquartered.

The senior officers of the *Arbiter* had fallen for Earthlings. More people were pair-bonding with Earthlings every day. Sorca had been defeated in challenge, which Ari still could hardly believe. But the most unbelievable of all…

"A Scorpiian bounty hunter." He had to say the words out loud. It just seemed too insane when he repeated them in his head.

Ari would have thought it physiologically impossible for a Scorpiian to form an emotional bond with anyone—or to feel anything but cold, calculating assessment toward another lifeform, for that matter.

But then Ari had seen Zemanni and Brooke together. There was definitely something going on there, and it was anything but cold.

Vay and Henry were together, too, and that… That was

the one thing that made sense to him. Vay had been his best friend since they'd been assigned to the *Arbiter* together. He was glad to see her so happy. He just didn't know how long it would last.

One or two pair-bonds with Earthlings might be recognized. This many? It was unlikely.

It was much more probable that the High Council would order everyone's memories wiped and then change Earth's status from a preservation site to a banned planet, seeing it as a source of cultural contamination. And if Earth lost preservation status, the smugglers and invading species would arrive in earnest.

He felt a pang for the Earthlings if that came to pass. What his fellow soldiers and the Department of Homeworld Security were doing was dangerous. In bonding as they tried to protect Earth, they could be opening it up to even more dangers.

At the same time, Ari couldn't stop wondering what it must be like for them. How deep must their connections be that they were willing to sacrifice so much to be together? And what was it about this planet that was making people he'd known and served with for decades suddenly make such huge changes?

He had a feeling these were just the initial ripples of a huge change that was coming to the Coalition whether it was ready for it or not. When all was done, he didn't know if his friends would find more happiness or if they would

lose everything they'd found. He didn't know how to help
—them or himself.

"Ari."

He turned at the strong female voice behind him. Kira.
She was standing in the doorway, arms loose at her sides.

"I have a mission for you," she said. "There's a reading
coming in from Florida and I need you to check it out."

"Of course." His heart pounded strongly, his throat
suddenly dry.

Missions are what had started most of these
relationships for the others. What if he met someone, too?
What if the strange effect of Earth crept over him and—

"Ari?"

He shook himself. "Yes?"

"Were you listening?"

"I'm sorry, sir. I was lost in thought for a moment. You
have my full attention now."

A crease appeared between her dark brows. "Good,
because you're going to need your full attention for this
mission. The readings are unlike anything we've seen
before. Could be a lead on the Centauri base, could be
something new."

"I'll run it down, sir."

"We leave in two hours."

He followed her as she turned and strode down the hall.
The Tau Ceti had obtained technology that was beyond
anything they had encountered. General Serath—Adam—

had taken what survived their encounters onto the *Arbiter* for analysis and to help him make his case with the High Council.

If there was more technology of that level on Earth, Ari would certainly need his wits about him. And yet...

He couldn't stop thinking about his fellow soldiers. At the way they looked at their mates, the way they always seemed to gravitate toward each other, even without realizing it.

Before the huge change hit them, he wondered if perhaps he might get a taste of that happiness for himself after all.

—

Everyone around Ari is falling for Earthlings. His fellow Coalition soldiers, even the ruthless Scorpiian assassin. He doesn't know what to make of all this pair-bonding...until he meets Sarah. Read on for a sneak peek at *Duel Citizenship.*

Duel Citizenship

The Department of Homeworld Security
Book Six

Chapter One

"This planet's diversity is remarkable." Ari checked the readouts on his screen again. The geological scans were returning data he wasn't sure he was interpreting correctly. "Are we really hovering over a sandbar? That people *live* on?"

Kira smiled. "Earthlings are innovative, especially considering the level of their technology. Perhaps because of it. They're unable to build space stations that can support large numbers of people and don't have the technology to make dome worlds. They have to make do with what they have, and the planet is heavily populated."

"Yet they still leave vast areas untouched." He wished he could see more through the viewports, but the sky was still dark.

"That's a good thing. They're already starting to understand the importance of managing their resources." Her smile faded. "And we need to help them stay on the right path—especially once they find out about us."

"Understood." Ari turned his attention back to his scans with more focus.

Someone was using advanced technology nearby. Technology that rivaled—if not surpassed—that of their own scout ship. Kira kept the vessel steady, hovering high above one of the smaller cities in the region while Ari tried to pinpoint the source.

"I can't get the source of the reading narrowed down to more than a few miles radius," he said. "I think we need to move in closer."

"We only have twenty minutes till the sun rises. I need to be back at headquarters by then."

"I'm detecting a stretch of road near the area of interest that isn't heavily traveled. If you drop me off there, I can investigate further."

"You'll need to set up a base of operations. You'll be here for days and will have to interact with Earthlings."

"Yes, sir."

She didn't respond at first, except to scowl as her brow

furrowed. "Are you sure you're up for this? Earth can be... bewildering."

"I've been acclimating for months. All of us have."

And yet it was still strange to see his commanding officer wearing Earth clothing—jeans and a light sweater. Her dark brown hair was in a loose ponytail instead of the regulation bun that was required when she was in uniform. If their scout ship malfunctioned, they needed to be able to blend in with the Earthlings of the area. Their shining silver uniforms would not help with that.

Ari's outfit was designed to match the culture of this region of the continent. They had anticipated the possibility that he would need to scout out the area.

Brendan, Kira's Earthling bondmate, had insisted that Ari wear ridiculous shoes called "loafers". They barely felt like shoes at all, especially compared with the boots he was used to. Apparently, wearing heavier shoes in the warm climate of Florida would make him stand out, even during their early spring season.

As if the shoes weren't bad enough, he was also wearing a brightly colored button-down shirt that was decorated with what was called a "tropical pattern" and pale tan shorts that barely reached his knees.

At least the shorts had plenty of pockets.

He was supposed to look like a tourist so that anyone who noticed he was out of place wouldn't think too hard about him. Brendan had packed a duffle bag with everything Ari should need for his mission. Money, clothing, identification cards.

The watch Ari wore integrated Coalition technology with Earth's in an inconspicuous form—another innovation from Brendan, though with the help of Coalition engineers. In addition to being a communication device, it could act as a small scanner, letting Ari covertly search for the alien technology he was looking for.

He had to admit, the Planetary Liaison had chosen well in pair-bonding with Brendan, even if she had done it for something as irrational as love.

"This isn't going to be like interactions at the mansion," Kira said. "You've been spending time with specific Earthlings in the controlled setting of our headquarters—which is in a radically different ecosystem from this one."

That was true enough. It was hard to believe that they had flown from mountains covered in snow to the sub-tropical setting around them on the same planet. He'd been on worlds with variations in their ecosystems, of course, but planets with diversity as extreme as Earth's were rare.

Once more, he wished they could fly during daylight so that he could see the change in vegetation with his own eyes instead of scanner readouts. Coalition protocol dictated that all in-atmosphere flights had to take place at night, even when their ship was cloaked.

Kira watched him silently, lips pulled in a concerned frown.

"I can handle it, sir," Ari said.

She nodded curtly, maneuvering the ship toward the road he had pointed out, then setting it down in a gentle landing. He released the clamp that kept his chair still and swiveled around to face the back of the small ship.

"The ground will shift beneath your feet," she said.

He paused in unfastening his safety harness. "Excuse me?"

"I read your file. You've spent most of your time aboard ships and stations."

"That's right."

"You're about to step onto a sandbar. When you walk on sand, it moves."

He smiled, trying to reassure her—and himself. "I'll do my best not to fall."

"See that you don't." She was grimacing again, dark eyes narrowed. "This mission—what we're doing here— it's important. We have no idea how many alien species have invaded Earth. If we can't get this under control, the High Council may revoke the preservation status for the planet and bring it into the Coalition."

He nodded. "And Earth isn't ready for that. I understand."

"I'm not sure that you do. But you will, after you spend some time here." She smiled faintly. "Enjoy it while you can."

"Yes, sir."

"Check in every three hours outside of your rest cycle. Dismissed."

He half-crawled out of the chair, keeping his body hunched over as he grabbed his bag. Kira opened the hatch and a ramp slid out from within the ship's hull, which had decloaked to help Ari make his way outside.

He had to turn sideways to exit the ship, bypassing the short ramp and stepping out with one foot on the road while ducking to maneuver the rest of his body through the opening. Most Sadirians were genetically engineered to be small and wiry. Living on dome worlds and space stations, creating citizens who were bigger was considered a waste of resources. Of course, accidents happened—like Ari.

His size had bothered him until he'd been assigned to the *Arbiter*. The first time he'd watched General Serath— the highest ranking military officer in the Coalition's fleet —do the same twisting maneuver to exit a tiny scout ship was the first time Ari had actually felt proud to be a glitch.

He was in good company, at least, especially aboard the *Arbiter*. Most of the crew were glitches. Serath's first officer, Khel, was even bigger than Ari, though not by much.

The *Arbiter* had been the first place that had felt like home.

Being among the team assigned to find and contain the aliens who were trespassing on Earth was a huge show of Serath's trust. Ari still sometimes wished that he had remained with the crew when the ship went back to Sadr-4 to try to convince the High Council to recognize Earth's First Contact committee, though.

Earth had a strange effect on his fellow Sadirians. General Serath had been the first to pair-bond with an Earthling, going so far as to change his name to "Adam Smith", not that Ari had been able to start thinking of him that way yet. *Adam* wore his hair differently, carried himself differently, and seemed to have been fundamentally changed by his experiences on Earth.

As if that wasn't enough, Kira had bonded with Brendan. Sorca with Eric. Moons, even Khel had bonded with Brendan's sister, Paige. And then Vay had fallen for an Earthling named Henry.

The others in their small team were already talking about possibly bonding with an Earthling. Most were excited, after seeing how happy their fellow soldiers were with their chosen partners. And it wasn't just the Sadirians who were bonding.

The Scorpiian that they'd been hunting for months had fallen in love with an Earthling and pair-bonded with her. Ari still couldn't believe the cold-blooded assassin now smiled and laughed—and even went on missions alongside the team. At least, when he wasn't busy playing video games or "spending quality time" with his bondmate.

Zemanni had actually been able to convince the pair of Lyrians living at headquarters that he'd changed. That was a good thing, since the female—Barbara—had been eager to tear him apart *again* when he first showed up.

It was a lot to wrap his head around.

Ari trotted away from the scout vessel as the hatch closed and the ramp retracted. Kira swung the ship around, nodding to him through the main viewport. A rippling wave passed over the ship's hull as it vanished.

He felt a slight turbulence in the air as it took off, heading back for headquarters. She'd be back with her own Earthling bondmate before Ari made it to the town. Especially if he didn't get moving.

Kira's warning about the shifting sands had unnerved him a bit. The road was solid, at least. He crossed to the edge, using the pre-dawn light to note where the dark material ended and the white-tan sand began. Stabilizing himself on one leg, he poked his free foot over the edge.

The sand barely gave any resistance at first. He had his shoe buried up to the toe before he had to apply pressure to dig deeper.

A blaring, discordant noise behind him made him jump forward, trying to spin on the soft surface. He flailed his arms to keep his balance, ending in a fighting crouch. The car that had made the awful noise kept speeding down the roadway.

Ari needed to be more careful. He would get plenty of practice walking on sand as he made his way toward the town. He checked his watch once more before setting out.

—

About the Author

USA Today Bestselling author Cassandra Chandler uses her vivid imagination to make the world more interesting, spawning the ideas she turns into her whimsical Science Fiction romcoms and darkly evocative Paranormal and Urban Fantasy Romances. Fast-paced and funny, lighthearted or dark, her stories will introduce you to characters you want to be friends with and worlds where you'd like to build a vacation home.